HIRED KILLERS
MEET THEIR FATE!

"God almighty," somebody murmured.

Clint Adams removed his Stetson and readjusted it on his head.

The two bodies lying on the floor each had a single bullet hole—one in the heart, the other in the throat.

The Gunsmith stood in the center of the barroom now, having holstered his six-gun.

"Anybody else have anything to say?" he asked. . . .

THE GUNSMITH

119

ARIZONA AMBUSH

J. R. ROBERTS

JOVE BOOKS, NEW YORK

ARIZONA AMBUSH

A Jove Book / published by arrangement with
the author

PRINTING HISTORY
Jove edition / November 1991

ISBN: 0-515-10710-7

Jove Books are published by The Berkley Publishing Group,
200 Madison Avenue, New York, New York 10016.
The name "JOVE" and the "J" logo
are trademarks belonging to Jove Publications, Inc.

PRINTED IN THE UNITED STATES OF AMERICA

10 9 8 7 6 5 4 3 2 1

THE GUNSMITH

119

ARIZONA AMBUSH

ONE

Keeping his horse Duke to the narrow trail's steep lift, Clint Adams climbed out of the deep socket of the canyon toward the high, lush meadows and timbered benches of the high country, to be met by the cooling wind as it reached down from the Mooncup Hills, all the way to the great stretch of the plains.

It was new country to the Gunsmith, and he was enjoying it. And he was anticipating seeing Hank Denzel, an old sidekick he'd ridden with for the Hoodoo outfit down on the Tensleep River. Hank hadn't written—he barely knew how to write—but he sure knew how to draw his 'letter'. Crowded into the envelope were a number of his sketches of his ranch and the surrounding country; horses, cattle, the land . . . but mostly Clint had been struck by the drawing of a hanged man. Another sketch was a horse, saddled and bridled, but with no rider. The horse was looking off into the distance, as though listening; its ears were up, and Hank, the artist, had caught exactly the alert tone of the animal. Clint had the feeling

1

that the animal was either waiting for his rider, or had lost him. And that was how Hank's sketches always appeared. Not saying anything directly, but questioning, as though calling for something more from the viewer.

Duke, the big, clean-limbed black gelding, had been leaning well into the rise of the hills. Now he broke stride and blew, swinging his head with bit and bridle jangling, and saddle leather creaking, as Clint shifted his weight.

"What you got, boy?" Clint asked, aware that the big horse had sensed something up ahead of them. He stood in his stirrups now and searched the trail, and especially the sharp rise ahead; listening to the ticking land, the breath of slight stirring wind, warm on his face and hands now, no longer cool and refreshing.

Now the trail crossed a narrow bench, mounted a short rise and rounded a thicket of bullberry bushes, some jackpine and spruce, and some cottonwood. And then all at once, they broke into a clearing. At the same time Clint felt the wariness of Duke—so attuned were horse and rider. Duke's big neck arched and his ears flattened out to the sides. He snorted and blew again, and began to walk as though crossing ice, while his rider keened to every sound stirred by the new and still slight wind that blew along the suddenly boney trail. And then it was suddenly there, in full view. At the same time the stench hit him.

The Gunsmith had seen hanged men; always a grim spectacle. Nor was the present moment eased by having witnessed it before. In this case the man had been hanging long enough for the buzzards to have feasted. And in fact, as Clint kicked the reluctant Duke forward, two dark, gloomy and funereal figures

rose with beating wings from the shadows thrown by
the tall cottonwood, flapping and croaking, clearly
annoyed at the intruder interrupting their feast.

The stench was bad enough for Clint to tie his
bandanna around his nose and mouth. And then he
saw the paper hammered into the tree with bullets.

"Warning! To all horse thieves. This body will be
yours if you steal a horse in Willow County."

Clint had been about to cut the body down, but
thought better. Whoever had hanged the man and
shot that note into the cottonwood tree might still be
somewhere about, in which case he would be seen as
interfering with the warning. He took a quick survey
of the small clearing as a beam of sunlight anchored
onto the dead man hanging like a dirty sack on the
end of the brand new manila lariat rope.

A nice touch, the Gunsmith reflected, wondering
whose dry courtesy had selected a new rope for the
job while he rode through the little clearing—the
grisly odor stinging his eyes, his hands, his whole
self—and at last out into the clean, young meadow
beyond.

And reflecting, as he rode, that the person who had
written the note was evidently educated. Such warn-
ings were usually scribbled and often barely literate.
He had the cold feeling that the hanging had more
than a little to do with Hank Denzel.

He had decided to skirt the edge of the meadow,
and so rode slowly, still partially protected by the trees
and some shrubbery. He wasn't sure anyone would be
about, for the hanging had taken place some while ago,
judging by the condition of the victim; still, he didn't
lose his caution. In the high country watchers were
always a possibility.

Now the blue sky was swept totally clear; there wasn't even the wisp of a cloud, while the green meadow was empty save for a single pronghorn antelope at the far edge. It was standing there, obviously questioning the intrusion of the man and horse, and Clint Adams clearly felt the royalty of the soft, graceful animal. In the next moment it was gone, following the others of its band into the shelter of thick foliage.

Although he was still sure no one was near, Clint rode around the edges of the meadow and not across it. Then he decided to follow the tracks of the antelope. These led him along a thin trail over which much game had passed, but no horses.

In a few more moments the trees began to thin and then—it seemed sudden—he was through and out in the clear, drawing rein on the edge of a high escarpment overlooking a wide valley, from across which great rimrocks reflected the amber light of the morning sun.

To his right, across a cut in the edge of the escarpment a great crag of dark stone arose like a monument to the sky. It stood there naked, waiting for the morning light to warm it.

Clint shifted in his saddle to look more closely at the valley, lifting his field glasses as he did so. The valley was deep, with a river running through it, and right away he spotted the cabin on the far side. It wasn't a large cabin. It was built of logs; and there was, too, a round horse corral, some dotted cattle, and what looked to be a barn and another building, likely a bunkhouse. There were three horses in the corral. Smoke was curling up from the cabin chimney. From Hank Denzel's drawings it had to be his place. He saw a dog walking slowly toward the watering trough, and a box wagon with its rear end jacked up, evidently in need of repair. But no sign of people.

Down river, he picked up another spread, but a good deal larger; and still farther down, just ahead of some foothills, a town.

It had to be Wingtree. He turned the glasses again onto Hank Denzel's spread, but there was still no sign of anyone. He had just put the glasses back in their case when he became sharply aware of something off to his right side. Instantly alert, he turned his head, ready for anything with his hand dropping to his holstered six-gun.

There, at the very summit of the tall, lonely crag he had spotted when he first rode onto the escarpment, stood a huge Rocky Mountain sheep. It stood absolutely without moving, its four feet together as one on the pinnacle. Its magnificent shaggy head and great rounded horns seemed carved into the azure sky. Clint had seen these rare animals on only a few occasions, and again he was at once struck by the regality and the absolutely still attention that revealed a power he knew could suddenly move like lightning. The animal was motionless externally, but Clint knew its awareness was as keen as light while it regarded the great distance before him, the endless sky, supremely confident in his domain, where only nature was greater than he.

Clint realized he must have blinked, for suddenly the sheep was gone. Vanished from the sight of the intruder. The Gunsmith sat his horse in total stillness now; the kind of stillness that was like stone on the outside, but within carried a force similar to that of the great sheep. The moment that had held him in thrall was gone, but its effect was still present. Then, realizing the need for another kind of attention, he kneed the big black horse, laying the reins alongside his neck to guide his direction, and began humming a song under his breath, one that he'd heard long ago down in Old Meeteetse on the Greybull river.

In the very nick of time the Gunsmith caught the glint of sunlight on metal; and he was out of the saddle and rolling, his Colt in his fist, his eyes still holding the place from which the warning shot had come.

He lay flat out, hugging the hard ground, drawing all the protection he could from the clump of sage and a rock; his eyes first quickly taking in the terrain up ahead, and as far to the sides as he could see without moving, then letting his vision move slowly over the same area. Was he flanked? He was not sure. He'd have to play it like he was. For sure, the man up ahead, behind the deadfall at the edge of the canopy of foliage that gave him the advantage of shade, was not shooting on the run. He was there to stay. And he had the advantage of elevation.

Clint felt the hot sun on his back and he knew that it was going to be there a long while. He told himself he might as well have been lying on a pool table. He would have given plenty to have the Winchester that was sitting snug in its scabbard, butt forward, alongside Duke's shoulder. There was no chance of his making a run for it. Before he'd get to his feet the dry gulcher would get him. And even if he did make it, Duke would more than likely catch lead.

He would have to wait. That shot had come too damn close for him to risk a run for the trees. He just hoped the killer was alone. And he began to wonder what sort of man it was. Someone who'd been backtrailing him? Or was it an outrider for one of the cow outfits? Or just some ornery homesteader type, protecting his range?

While these thoughts were running through him, he was trying to calculate the other man's exact position. He too would likely be lying on his belly, judging by the size of that clump of sagebrush. Not a smart move, actually, shooting without first being sure of good cover, like that line of rock off to the right.

Just then he heard the horse coming up on his left, blowing a couple of times. The rider would be coming off the trail that fed through the fir and spruce. The question was whether the visitor was connected with the rifleman up ahead.

He had twisted his body as much as he could without exposing himself to the gulcher above him, so that he could sight on the spot where he knew the horseman would come. Meanwhile, the sweat was pouring into his eyes, and his shirt was clinging to him. Carefully he wiped his hands on some sagebrush beside him. A loose grip was not what he needed right now.

It was a little chestnut horse that came off the game trail through the spruce and fir and onto the spread of buffalo grass and sage. Clint was watching closely, with half his attention on the rifle up ahead of him. Perhaps the biggest surprise was seeing that the rider was not at all what he had pictured. It was a woman. A young woman. A beautiful young woman. But his awe was short-lived; it was no time for indulgence. And his next thought was whether the bushwhacker would also take a shot at the girl; who, he noted swifter than thought, couldn't have been more than an early twenty-some. But his amazement had already turned to astonishment as he saw the Henry rifle she was holding across the pommel of her saddle.

Then he was rolling, as the man above him shouted something and the bullet from his rifle sliced the atmosphere right next to Clint's head. But now the Gunsmith was up on his knees and had shot the bushwhacker in the shoulder. The man let out a screaming curse as he dropped his rifle.

The Gunsmith was all the way up now, standing in a half crouch covering the would-be killer as well as the girl, who hadn't moved; only her chestnut pony had taken two steps, spooked some at the firing, but the girl had controlled him, her face pale, and Clint could see she was biting her lip. Yet she hadn't moved her rifle; it remained across the pommel of her stock saddle, while her grip had tightened on her reins.

The man who had tried to shoot Clint was standing up, holding his shoulder, looking sheepish and angry at the same time. He must have been younger than the girl.

"Johnnie, are you all right?" She had kept her eyes on Clint while she called.

"I am all right. Just got my arm near shot off, for Chrissake!"

"John! I don't want to hear language like that! How many times . . ." But she caught herself and stared at the Gunsmith.

"Mister . . ." And Clint could detect the quiver behind her words. "I don't know what you're doing up here, but this is Bar Z summer range. That is why my brother took a shot at you."

"I was sure wondering why," Clint said, his tone dry as dust. "Somebody better teach him how to fire a warning shot. The idea is to haze a man off, not damn near blow him away."

"He didn't hit you, did he?" Now he caught her concern, and it was sincere.

"I reckon only a young fool could come that close and miss both me and my horse," the Gunsmith said. And then, with a lightning move he holstered the six-gun. "I didn't see any notice that this here was private range, Miss. As far as I am concerned, the western range is for anyone takes a notion to ride it."

"That is the way it used to be—yes. But not now." She had drawn closer to him as he walked toward Duke and he was checking his rigging while he talked.

"I'd allow you have got range troubles," he said, more as statement than question. And he stopped checking his stirrup strap and stood there looking squarely at her high cheekbones, hazel eyes and superb figure; especially as she took a deep breath and her bosom swelled under her calico blouse. But he quickly brought himself back to the business at hand.

"Miss, I am just riding through. I wasn't figurin' on cutting any fence or stealing any horses or beeves."

"You could have killed him," she said, facing him squarely now.

"I could have, except I didn't intend to. I hit him to disarm him, Miss. I don't believe he's fixing to die just yet."

She started to say something to that, but her brother cut her off.

"Sis, I can handle this. I'm all right. Let's drop it."

"I want to see that arm," she said, dismounting now. And the Gunsmith had a moment of admiring her buttocks under her tight riding breeches.

Clint had reached into his saddle bag and taken out a piece of an old shirt which he kept for just such emergencies as this one. "Here, you can use this."

He walked over to where the two were standing and handed it to the girl who, taking it, looked at him, murmuring a thank you of some sort or other as she flushed and turned back to her brother.

But Clint Adams had felt the moment; her look had gone through him like a branding iron, and he felt the throb in his trousers.

She had helped the boy pull away his shirt. It was a flesh wound. Painful, as his attitude showed, and his reluctance to his sister's ministrations was quite clear. "I will do it," he said.

"One-handed!"

"Damn!"

But he stood still while she wrapped the cloth around his shoulder and upper arm.

"That's a little too tight," Clint said.

"I want to control the bleeding."

"You can only slow it. I don't think I hit the bone, or he wouldn't be standing there so friendly like. You need it tight, but you don't want to cut the circulation. Is it far to your outfit?"

"Not far." She was busy wrapping the bandage again, while her brother stood there, fuming silently like a prisoner wrongly accused.

Clint liked him. He saw that the boy couldn't have been more than maybe seventeen, eighteen. And he saw too that under their apparent bickering the two were essentially fond of each other.

"You a nurse, Miss? You did that real nice." He smiled at the side of her face.

Without turning her head she said, cool as a plate of spring water, "I am glad you approve, sir. I am rather good at following instructions—I've been told."

She had finished with the bandage now and suddenly with a happy little laugh leaned forward and gave her brother a peck on his cheek. He jerked away, but not in time; his face was dark with irritation.

"Now, come on, Johnnie. Don't have to be ashamed of a sister giving you a little love peck."

"Ugh!" With his free hand he reached up and ran his sleeve over his face.

While peals of laughter fell from his sister as she put her arm around him and hugged.

"Take it slow on that arm!" he said. But Clint could see he wasn't all that reluctant.

"Is your outfit nearby?" Clint asked.

"We're just across the river." And then after studying him for a moment, she said, "Come by. It's getting time for dinner."

"Obliged," Clint said. And he touched the brim of his Stetson hat with his fore- and middle fingers.

And then it suddenly dawned on him. He had felt something during the bandage wrapping, but now it was more clear.

"I am looking for a man name of Hank Denzel," he said. "I do believe his spread is hereabouts."

The color had left her face so suddenly, it was almost as though from a blow. And Clint Adams felt something twist in his guts.

"You're his; you're related," he said, saying it with difficulty, for he felt the dread building in him as he watched their faces.

"Then, you are . . ." The girl didn't finish the sentence, and he saw the tears standing in her eyes.

"I'm Clint Adams."

"I almost shot you," the boy said, his voice sounding hollow.

The girl brushed some loose hair out of her eyes and said, "Dad is dead." Her tears hadn't left her eyes. They stood, one in each corner; like a jewel, Clint thought, as the sun touched her face.

But she had paled suddenly. "He's been dead less than a little while. He was hoping, wanting you to come."

"I didn't know it was . . ."

"Of course," she said. "Dad never wanted to burden anyone with anything."

They stood there then in their silence. Clint's thoughts were running, trying to piece something together.

"My name is Maggie," the girl suddenly said. She turned toward her brother, and when he didn't speak she said, "This is Johnnie."

Clint was silent.

The girl said, "We live across the river."

"I know. Hank drew me a picture in his letter. And I spotted the place with my field glasses just before riding up here."

Again they fell silent, while Clint checked Duke's cinch.

"Will you ride back with us then?" Maggie asked.

He didn't answer her. He said, "You know, I was just thinking something."

"What?"

"I'll bet you're as good at building a pot of coffee as you are at bandaging shoulders."

TWO

"I guess we were both in Dakota in school when you knew Dad," Maggie was saying as the three of them sat around the kitchen table with coffee and baking powder biscuits.

"Hank never mentioned family much. I only knew his wife had died which was why he was down around Meeteetse working for the Arbuckle outfit. I never knew he had kids. But . . ." He paused, and he saw how closely they were listening to him.

"Funny, I always felt he had something."

"Some thing?" Maggie asked, spacing the two words.

Clint spent a moment looking for the right way to put it. "Like, well, it was like he was a happy man. I don't mean he was always busting out laughing, but it was—well, like he had something, somewhere, stashed away. I figure it must have been the both of you."

Maggie gave a little laugh of pleasure. "I know

what you mean. Dad was like that. Quiet sort of. I don't know."

"Were you long in Dakota?"

"Couple of years." Johnnie stood up. "I want to take a look at the rimrocks again," he said. "There's been long riders about. That's why I shot at you." His face was taken over by his sheepish look once again.

"How long has this been going on?" Clint asked. "And you'd better rest that arm."

"It's been going on since Dad was shot. Well, actually before. But not so much out in the open," Maggie said.

"The Stringer outfit wanted to buy this place," Johnnie said, turning back from the door and sitting again at the table. "Not only didn't Dad want to sell, but their price, their offer, was crazy."

"Which you, or Hank anyway, turned down."

Maggie said, "They shot at Dad twice. The first time he got away. He was riding fence. The second time he was hit in the leg when he was riding along the Greyhorn Trail. That's a thin trail way high up and they winged him, then shot his horse and he went over the side."

"Only a few days later Harvey Stringer came by with his offer," Johnnie said, taking up the story. "Course, we told him to git."

"Since then there has been fence cutting," Maggie continued. "Stampeding our horses. And even some calf rustling, but nothing we can prove. No person caught with a running iron in his hands. And then there's been rumors spreading around town that Dad borrowed money from old man Stringer and didn't pay it back."

"That was the simplest piece of lying," Johnnie said.

"Johnnie, we don't need to go into that!" Maggie's voice was sharp as she swiftly cut into her brother's account.

"How many Stringers are there?" Clint asked. "You mentioned two."

"There are five counting Pa Stringer; a pair of twins, Harvey and Matt, and then Cyrus and Pierce, and their father."

"I get the feeling they're a tough crew."

"Dad threw the five of them off the place about a year back," Johnnie said. He looked at his sister. "I bet that's how it got made worse. Those devils just couldn't handle being backwatered by Dad."

Clint had a chuckle at that. "I know how ornery Hank could be," he said ruefully. "He was no man to talk back to."

"They certainly didn't have the courage to talk back to his face," Maggie said. She lowered her head, then straightened.

Clint had walked to the front window of the cabin and now spoke without looking around. "We've got company."

Instantly the two were at his side.

"That's the twins," Maggie said. "Harvey and Matt."

Johnnie had picked up his Winchester and started toward the door.

"No, Johnnie!" And Maggie swept in front of her brother as they all heard the horses coming in fast.

But Clint Adams was ahead of both of them, blocking the door. "I owe you one, Johnnie, and besides, Hank was sort of asking me to help out."

Maggie started to say something, but he waved his hand at her. "You make a terrific bucket of coffee, Miss Denzel, but that doesn't mean you can gun down a pair like that. I'll handle this." And he opened the door and stepped outside of the cabin as the two riders pulled up, raising a sheet of dust that came almost up to their saddles, then banked slowly toward the door of the cabin.

They sat their bay horses and looked down at the man who was standing with his thumbs hooked into his gunbelt.

"Easy, Matt. Let himself start the talkin'."

They were hard, they were both bearded, and they were dusty. The sneers on their faces emphasized the fact that they were indeed twins.

But the Gunsmith didn't say anything. He simply stood there, now with his hands down from his belt, at his sides. Ready to draw.

"Cat got his tongue," one said.

His brother grinned. "Tell my girlfriend inside that Matthew is calling."

"Don't you have the guts to tell her yourself?"

Both Stringers slapped leather at the same time, only to find themselves staring into the hard, round hole that was the business end of the Gunsmith's Colt .45.

"Shit," said the one named Matt.

His brother Harvey was grinning. "We'll just have to get the feller when he ain't lookin' is how it's gonna have to be."

"Like you did Hank Denzel?"

"You a lawman, mister?"

"Cut for home, boys. But remember one thing. I don't like drawing my gun without using it. I do that maybe once every couple, three years. Like just for

practice. This time now is the 'once.' Next time . . .
well, if I was you I wouldn't let there be a next time.
Now git."

He watched them all the way out of sight. And then
he turned and walked back into the kitchen.

Johnnie's eyes were bugging out of their sockets
with excitement. "Holy Moses! You sure cut their
juice off, mister."

Clint turned to Maggie and said, "Miss, and you
too, Johnnie Denzel. I'm out of a job at the moment.
Wondered if you could use a extra hand about the
place."

"That would be wonderful, Mister Adams," Maggie said. "But we don't have any money. No money
at all."

"Miss Denzel, I didn't ask you for money. I asked
you for a job."

He watched the smile teasing the corners of her
lovely mouth.

"But you'll have to call me Maggie, and not be all
that formal." And then she added, "Clint?"

"Clint." And the Gunsmith added, "Reckon I could
handle another cup of that mighty fine java, Miss
Denzel?" And then seeing the scolding look come
into her face he said quickly, "Maggie."

"Tolt ya! God damn yer eyes. Din't I tolt ya!" The
old man's bullwhip cracked out and cut the cigar right
in half, leaving only a soggy, chewed butt in his son
Pierce's quivering jaw.

Old man Stringer stood tough and hard as a crowbar
in front of his four sons. Not only hard, but sharp of
tongue, and with a temper swifter even than that whip.
He had raised his brood to obey nobody but himself.

And none challenged that law. Only Pierce, the first
son, had just made that mistake. His father had taken
the whip to him, then an oaken club, and finally his
fists. Pierce was old Hannibal Stringer's favorite—
the eldest, the first son—but he had never been able
to beat the old man.

Right now he had managed to land one blow, a
tremendous right to the patriarch's jaw, cushioned
somewhat by the old man's furious, bespittled and
tobacco-strewn beard, but hard as Thor's hammer even
so. And the old man hadn't even taken a backward step.
Instead, he had readily accepted the challenge in his
eldest's insubordination and had dropped him with
a vicious kick in the crotch, followed by a wicked
rabbit punch on Pierce's eardrum.

While the remaining three brothers stared in awe
at this donnybrook between patriarch and possible
successor, Pierce struggled to his feet. Pa waited.

"I be gonna whip your ass, boy!"

Pierce, his right eye already darkly swollen, his
mouth a wet, scarlet smear, stood swaying before his
father, while his brothers watched.

"I gonna whip you to pieces! Don't you never dare
talk back to your ever-lovin' dad like that. You puppy!
Yeller-assed puppy!"

The whip cracked out and cut like a knife into
Pierce's arm. Pierce charged, still wobbly but game
all the way through, and the old man stepped easily
aside, tripping him and cutting the stock whip savagely
into his son's buttocks.

Not a sound came from the sons who stood locked
in awe at the spectacle. It was not rare. They had not
only seen it before, but each knew the receiving end
of it. The old man was unbeatable.

Three wicked cuts of the whip had torn Pierce's pants and the backs of his legs. Hannibal Stringer lifted the whip for one more cut, but then lowered his arm. His eyes were ablaze, looking to his sons like fiery coals.

They could see that their father was tired. He stood there, legs spread apart, the whip loose in his gnarled hand, breathing extra, whistling a little as his tobacco breath came out of his pursed lips.

"Spare you that last one. Shows I got heart for you, boy. But you better know how lucky you be. You don't deserve sparing. You don't deserve nothin'. None of yez!" He glared at his other offspring. "Shit, a man can't settle his old age in peace, by the Lord,'thout his worthless issue fuckin' everythin' up and hurtin' the one what raised 'em from a litter, from snot-nosed, dirty-assed pups to men, by God. And what thanks does he git? Bringin' their old dad to the end of the trail in sorrer!" He staggered to the table and grabbed the bottle out of which all had been generously drinking, and tilted it into his mouth.

Choking, coughing, spitting and trying to swear he dropped it, but Harvey miraculously caught the precious object in the nick of time.

Meanwhile, his garbled accusation had hardly been heard by his sons, who had been the victims of such declarations of rage and self-pity ever since they'd been old enough to take any of it in.

"Boy, Pierce is sure sleepin' it off," observed Cyrus, the shortest, but also the widest of the brood.

But their sire was not through. He stood now, having regained the bottle, gripping it in his fist as he swayed before them. Triumphant in battle, yet soaked in sorrow for the foul treatment he had received from his worthless sons over the years.

For a moment his terrible eyes cleared. "Grown men—huh! Damn fools, going in there to the Bar Z. I should be whippin' you, the pair of you two, by Jesus! Not poor old Pierce, though he shoud'na' talked back. Damn fool knows how you shouldn't never talk back to your Paw." He stood close to the still prone Pierce, looking down out of those cold, grey, fish-like eyes. "Trouble always was, you was your Maw's favorite, being first. God damn sissy, she made ya."

Matt Stringer looked at his twin, Harvey, and suddenly screwed up some courage. "Paw, Maw ain't here now."

"I know that, you puppy! Goddamit. Didn't I mourn for her moren' the whole useless pack of yez!"

Then suddenly, out of nowhere it seemed, Cy spoke. "Paw . . ."

The scraggled grey head turned. "You thinkin' ye'll talk back too . . . ! Why, I'll . . ."

"Paw!" Spoken with a sudden and at the same time, strange softness, the word seemed to slip into the cabin room.

Hannibal Stringer looked at his youngest son, and a strange, quizzical expression entered his carved face.

"Paw, you tolt us that railroad feller was comin' out. I do believe I hear somethin'." Cyrus had crossed to one of the windows that opened onto the approach to the big Stringer outfit.

"What you see, boy?"

They all heard it now, the sound of a horse blowing and a man's voice giving orders.

"It's him," Cyrus said from the window. "That feller."

"By God, then, he better for sure brought with

him what he promised," snapped Hannibal Stringer, suddenly stone sober and all business as he crossed to the window to have a look. "Somebody clean up this mess here, real fast-like!"

Behind him, as his tight hard back blocked the window, his son Pierce struggled to his feet, and brother Matt handed him the bottle, from which he took a generous swig.

The old man turned back from the window. "It ain't the railroad feller, you knothead. It's . . . shit! It's old leather-ass Rhodes."

"What I want to do right now, gentlemen, is read you this piece from the newspaper."

The speaker was a soft, round man with a round belly, looking almost as though a medicine ball had been stuffed into his pants, rather large and rosy cheeks, almond colored eyes, and puffy hands with dimples where knuckles would have been. In a word, Elijah Soames was fat. Yet, strangely, he moved with an almost alarming grace. Alarming because it was so surprising to see such flowing movement in what at first glance so often appeared as mere fat, and supposed inertia. Mr. Elijah Soames was anything but inert. He moved with a fluidity that dancers would have envied, had a will of iron of which a judge might have been proud, and between his close-set eyes there lay a mind that could out-think, out-maneuver, out-scruple any politician, gambler or man-of-God.

Elijah leaned back in his chair now, raising his short arms to fold open the newspaper. Suddenly, he stood up to adjust his pants which were binding him— as they often did—in the crotch. Then he reseated himself with care. While he came from a family

of tall men and women—his two brothers and his
father were six feet and over—Elijah was five feet
nothing.

"Here we are!" He had licked his thumb in order
to open the page more easily. "Here we are." He
cleared his throat—he had a very short neck—and
began to read.

"It is estimated that the population—and this is giv-
en as an example—of Wingtree, a town lying almost
directly in line between Laramie and Reno is fifty
men, eight women, four boys, and six girls. Besides
this there are nineteen horses, probably mostly geld-
ings, and some thirty to thirty-five dogs, and a few
cats. Already, it has been reported to this paper that
following the completion of only the sixth or seventh
house in Wingtree the whole population—minus the
children, it may possibly be supposed—came together
in one of the six saloons and elected a council. The
council is presently deciding whether to call Wingtree
a town or a city. Whatever; they are committed to
electing a mayor and whatever other officers might
be necessary in order to establish an honest government."

He lowered the paper, folded it; but when one of
the three men seated around his desk made as if to
reach for it, he slipped it swiftly into his desk drawer,
as though he hadn't seen the gesture.

"Gentlemen!" The voice was soft, cultured, and
knew well ahead what it was going to say. "Wonderful, is it not, the speed with which the great western
land is rebuilt—I say *rebuilt*—to meet the demands
of manifest destiny! The great hills are cut, roads are
graded, then ties and rails are laid down. And this
excitement, gentlemen, goes on all day long and all

night. Thus!" He held high a short, puffy index finger, stabbing it aloft as though ready to lead the legions to the promised land. Which as a matter of fact, was how Elijah Soames saw his role.

"And you will see, gentlemen, that with the railroad Wingtree will boom; Wingtree will be on the map; Wingtree will have a voice in the Territory; perhaps one day, even a voice in the nation. I assure you, gentlemen, it has happened just like that many times. Look at Ellsworth, look at Dodge, Abilene, and so many others." He leaned foward onto the desk, a generous roll of pink flesh escaping his tight collar and curving over the ring of perspiration on the top of his shirt.

There were three men seated before him. None of them even remotely resembled Elijah Soames. These were lanky men, long in the West, though not with cattle or sheep; rather, with commerce. Josiah Boles, Rick Hemming, and Tom Swindown, the principal citizens in town.

"You see," Elijah continued, "that Wingtree is already, today, no longer the nineteen-horse town it was only a short while ago. And so you can imagine what it will be with the railroad."

"Railroad means money for shipping," Tom Swindown pointed out, "not passenger travel. Freight. What we gonna ship?"

Elijah's pudgy lips appeared to grin. He opened his small hands. "Cattle!"

"Cattle! But we've not only got no railroad, but also no shipping facilities, and why the hell would any Texan in his right mind give a second thought to Wingtree as a shipping point! He'd be crazy as a hoot owl." This was Josiah Boles speaking, whose hardware store stood at the corner of Main Street and Copper Alley.

"There's beef around here," said Swindown, the town banker, a whip-lean man with a gravely wrinkled face. Some people suspected a breed background, for his face was nut-brown, and he sometimes had a wary look in his deep dark eyes. But the rumor kept below the surface, for Tom Swindown wielded the power of the purse, power of which there was none greater, at least in the neighborhood of Wingtree, and other points both east and west. "But we try something like that we'll have Stringer and his boys on our ass, and that's a gut!"

There followed a beat of silence, which Elijah did not fill, simply allowing his almond eyes to fall on the third gentleman, Richard "Rick" Hemming, Wingtree's man-of-God, undertaker, and legal advisor-in-residence. Rick was a stocky man with an eternally jovial expression on—though not in—his lean, narrow face. Close on either side of his beak-like nose, his greenish-yellow eyes protruded like small porcelain knobs. He was clean-shaven, though his wife—who shared a pact with him of speaking honestly to each other—often suggested that he grow a beard, claiming it would make "my husband" more distinguished, if slightly less genial. Rick Hemming was perfectly satisfied that he was already both, and in good measure.

Another moment of silence passed, while Elijah held his eyes on Hemming. Meanwhile, a lone ray of sunshine rode through the window pane that faced the street, and Elijah studied the dust dancing along it. He was thinking how it was necessary to order a special building to be constructed, a building that would house certain offices.

"It sounds like a good move to me," Rick Hemming was now saying. "Only not on the face of it. On the face of it, I agree with Josiah. We have enough cattle, for here-abouts that is, and why should we become shippers, with all the troubles and problems that a cowtown creates. Look at the trouble we've already got on our hands with horse stealing, and yes—beef rustling too." He paused. "But I feel that Elijah has something more on his mind than what he has been telling us." He grinned, and taking a bandanna out of his coat pocket dabbed at his forehead. "Seasonable, ain't it."

"It'll get hotter round noontime," Tom Swindown said.

"Shit-pisser," murmured Josiah Boles.

Now another silence fell into the drab, dubious-looking room. In fact, it was a barely-converted store-room in the back section of the No Return Saloon; loaned occasionally to patrons and others who could pay the price for gaming or meetings. Between times it was a catch-all room for leftover Fourth-of-July celebration banners, flags, firecrackers and other festivity equipment.

"Gentlemen, may I simply say that I have asked for this meeting with you to sound you out—firstly, on your feelings about Wingtree as a growing rather than a stagnating town. Look!" He held his thick forefinger higher this time to emphasize his point, then rose swiftly from his chair and took a turn around the room. "Look! There is only one way to win the West! One way to push back the frontier and wipe out the savages who deny Manifest Destiny. It is with people! With men, women, and children. People! Homes! Businesses! Schools!" He looked at Rick

Hemming. "Churches! Civilization, gentlemen, cannot be stopped. What I am saying is that if we do not take the bull by the horns, if we do not take the lead; then someone else surely will! We are, in a word, working in the service of progress, Manifest Destiny, the future of this Great Nation, working for our beloved country, and for God!" His head bowed as he stood at the edge of the table, his puffy knuckles just touching the edge. Rick Hemming was thinking how it could have been a pulpit. All were sitting now with heads bowed in cogitation over these, to them, surprising words. And yet, while they had not seen the situation in this way, they felt it to be true. Knew it was true!

"Wingtree could sure stand a little growing pains," allowed Josiah Boles.

"Well we are the town council," Rick Hemming said. "We are the leading citizens, and thus, we do have a responsibility. A big responsibility," he added. He cleared his throat; it sounded dry. His lips pursed in reflection. "After all's said and done . . ."

"There is going to be a railroad through this country," Soames cut in. "It is definite. The men, the money, the abilities are all committed. There is no turning back. It is coming, and nothing can stop it."

"The Injuns ain't gonna like it," Josiah Boles said.

"The natives," Rick Hemming said, folding his hands on the table in front of him, "must learn to listen to the will of the Lord! They must be educated. Then they will realize the benefits of our way of life, of civilization, the benefits that accrue to men who follow the path, the way to God!"

"Can you tell us more about the railroad?" Tom Swindown asked. Hemming and Boles had been watching him covertly since the question of Indians was raised, but Swindown showed no particular sign. Still, his business compatriots were wary. You never could tell. After all, blood was thicker than water, though good whiskey evened both. No, a man had to be careful.

"The railroad," Elijah said, raising his head with his chin forward. "The railroad could—I say it could— come through Wingtree. Though nothing is certain. Not at this stage. However, if there were certain inducements . . ." He shrugged, opened his hands. "Who knows?"

After a moment Boles asked, "Can anything be sure on it?" He had taken a cigar out of his coat pocket and now bit off the little bullet at the end.

"What then would be expected of us?" Hemming asked. "Of the council?"

Elijah had been leaning his elbows on the table and now he sat back in his chair, dropping his forearms as he opened his smooth hands.

"We can go into that at our next meeting. Gentlemen, if one of you would be kind enough to signal the bartender the refreshments will be on me."

THREE

That night at the Bar Z Clint had thrown his bedroll on the far side of the corral, just inside a strip of box elders. It seemed the best place for keeping a watch on things. He knew very well that he'd be hearing from those raunchy Stringer boys again. And that meant the Denzels would be getting it too.

So he had slept in his half-awake manner, the way he generally did on the trail. Twice during the night he got up and took a careful turn around the ranch house and outbuildings. But he heard nothing, saw nothing.

His last awaking was in the pre-dawn. This was the time—along with the evening just at twilight—that he liked best. The two twilights. Those singing moments at the beginning and ending of the day and night when he especially felt the the quiet authority of the land, the sky, and the wind. He stood watching the first light of the coming sun washing away the last of the nighttime, feeling the new warmth in his awakening body, and the fresh lift streaming through him.

Then he heard the door of the cabin open and close, but very quietly. It was almost without sound. And he knew it was her.

"You were so quiet I almost didn't hear you," he said, allowing her to come up behind him.

"I didn't want to wake Johnnie. Though he should be up soon anyway."

They were facing each other now in the soft morning, and he thought she was even more beautiful than the day before. Neither said anything as they simply looked into each other's eyes.

Finally she said, "What is it about eyes that is so wonderful?"

"I expect it's whose eyes you're talking about."

"Yours," she said boldly.

"And yours," he replied.

"It's wonderful."

"It's the best thing there is," Clint Adams said, slipping his arms around her.

Her lips were soft as air, and she gave them completely. At the same time her body melted into his. Standing there, weak from the strength of their overwhelming passion, Clint thought that all he wanted in the whole world at this moment was the girl in his arms.

"I want you more than anything," he said.

"I know. So do I. But . . ." Her breath burst against his eyelids as she moved back just a fraction, to catch a moment for herself.

"But what?" He kissed her on her nose, which had the loveliest curve upward at its tip. "Is it Johnnie?"

"We'd better wait till later." She leaned back in his arms, which were still circling her waist, so that she could look into his eyes. "Oh, I want you, I want you . . . !"

They had moved further into the protection of the trees. And now their lips pressed together again, while their tongues sought each other's.

"We do have to wait," Clint said. "There could be visitors about."

"No!" She stepped back and he let his arms come down. "You mean somebody might be here; at the ranch!"

"Why not? You saw them yesterday. They're not going to take that lying down. They'll be back."

She was staring at him with shock in her eyes, but now she melted into her earlier softness. Her eyes were glistening with joy as she looked up at him.

"You're right then. We're both right. We'll have to wait." She seemed to be thinking something then, with her thumb knuckle against her mouth. "But not for too long," she said, catching her breath.

"We can have a look about. What about your brother?"

"He's got his chores. I've got my work too. And . . ."

"And we'll find our time," Clint said. He paused. "Like 'long about after I'm done checking your range and all," he said with a slow grin.

Her eyes were dancing. "I just remember something."

"Yeah? What?"

"I remember that you're a man who likes a good, strong mug of coffee."

"I am," he said as they started toward the house. "And what do you favor, Miss?"

"You mean—especially?"

"Yup. 'Specially."

"You," she said, and as they walked to the house, close beside each other, her hand brushed his.

Clint felt his erection stronger than ever and had trouble banking that inner fire. But he knew the wisdom in picking the right moment and spot for lovemaking. And he knew the value of not rushing. And he knew that Maggie Denzel knew it too.

The sun was up as they walked around the corral heading for the back door of the cabin.

"Isn't it a wonderful morning?" she said, and she had a tone in her voice that Clint Adams hadn't yet heard.

"It sure is," he agreed. And then he said, "You know what's especially good about morning?"

"What? The lovely light?"

"That—yes. But there's something else."

They were at the door now and she had her hand on the knob as she half turned toward him. "Tell me."

"It's that you don't know what's going to happen."

And laughing lightly together they walked into the kitchen.

From a certain point of view, Clint Adams found it to be the longest day. Not that he had time on his hands. He had hardly enough time to do three-quarters of what he had figured to be necessary. He had decided first off, to ride fence along the north end of the Bar Z range, at the same time inspecting the Denzel stock, and making a count. And he also wanted to familiarize himself with the general layout of the Denzel spread. It all took the best part of the day, during the course of which his trail crossed one or both of the Denzels' and he was able to piece together more of their story. He was also able to gather more details on Hank; how he'd been living, and especially how he handled the troubles with the Stringers, and his difficulties with certain other ranchers, plus the bank, credit at the stores, and the general tenor of the Bar Z's neighbors. He also learned a few more things about Miss Maggie Denzel, all of which added up to the growing throb in his trousers.

Remembering Hank, Clint realized fully how he would have stood up to the Stringers and anyone else who had wanted to buy him out, or—as it finally came about—shoot him out. Yet, strangely, since the killing, when Hank had been shot at and his horse had taken him over the edge of the rimrock, there had been little threat from anyone, save the one visit of the Stringer twins. Yet neither Maggie nor her young brother felt that the trouble was ended. Other neighbors—the Wagners, John Millicombe, the Circle Slash outfit run by Fred Bell—though they had never actually threatened or pushed Hank Denzel overtly to sell out, they'd still made it known that he was not wanted. Yet, since his death, there had been no hostile sign from any of them.

"Likely, they're afraid of being accused of the shooting," Clint pointed out. "So they're laying low till things settle some. So we don't let our guard down."

This had been spoken about more freely at lunch which the three of them had shared high up above the Bar Z, on the top of a giant rock known as Fraunce's Peak. Maggie had told him the Peak was the best place for seeing the whole of that part of the country at a glance. It was all laid out in clean shapes, mostly told off by the color and shading of the land. It was easy to see from that height how vital Hank's place was to anyone driving cattle to the mountain, or as Clint realized as a possibility, to Wingtree.

"But Wingtree isn't any shipping point," Maggie pointed out.

"No, but it could be."

"There's no railroad."

"That could be a matter of time," Clint said. "You know those tracks get put down real fast."

"But why would anyone want to come to Wingtree? I mean, I like Wingtree, but I don't see it as any kind of place a lot of people would want to come to."

"Not now. But maybe some day. Once the railroad gets there, it could really go places."

"But why would anyone want to put a railroad here in the first place? We've got the stage to Lander and Laramie, and like that. There's no need for a train."

"Not now. I agree with that. But later."

"But who would use it?" she asked. "There aren't that many people."

"It could be used for shipping."

"Cattle?"

He grinned at her persistence. "Cattle, or whatever. See, the railroads aren't throwing all that money into construction just for the benefit of people."

"But there can't be that much cattle shipping. Or can there?"

"It works like this. You—say you're a railroad person. You get subsidized by the government. The government in Washington; they give you money to build a railroad, to open the land to immigrants from Europe and the eastern states, and also to push out the Indians. And they give land. The railroads build the towns as they go along, laying track, and meanwhile, for a song, they've been buying up more land all along where the track will be laid. You understand?"

"They get it both ways, is what you're saying. They're given money to build, to lay the rails and bring in the trains. And they've already bought up land along the track."

"Which they sell for a neat profit."

"And so they make money both ways."

"But what about the cattle shipments, you asked earlier," Clint continued. "You wanted to know about that."

"There can't be all that much cattle to ship. Certainly not around Wingtree."

"But there is in Texas." He watched her as she studied it. It was difficult not to be overcome by her good looks, which were revealed from every angle.

"Wow!" Maggie suddenly exclaimed. "They've thought of everything."

"They've got it covered both ways from the ace," Clint said.

She looked directly at him now. "I've got one last question. It seems to me that the whole of this area might get into this mess. Do you figure that's why somebody wants the Bar Z. Why Dad was . . . shot?"

He let a moment pass before speaking. Then he said, "I wouldn't be a bit surprised if that was so." He watched it hit her and after another moment he went on. "All that I've said is—maybe. Take it like that. It's what could, or what might happen. I can't say it will happen, or even that it is happening, because I don't know. I don't have any real evidence, facts. Anything that . . . well, that could be taken to law."

"I was just going to ask about the law," Maggie said.

"I don't guess there's a whole lot they can do. People running a big operation like that are good at covering up. They deal with towns like they were cards in a deck, people the same. The land speculators, the lawyers—watch it."

"Ah yes, I've heard about them," she said. "Dad used to speak about them selling poor land to the immigrants for big profit."

"There's more to it of course. But that's likely what you're up against, what Hank was up against. And for all I can tell, what Wingtree could be up against. I'm afraid it's a tough setup."

"Well then, maybe we should change the subject," she said.

It was at that moment that Johnnie Denzel re-appeared. He had left them there at the edge of the creek while he rode over to check the other side of the butte that was just to the east of the spot they had picked to rest their horses.

"I think we've about covered everything for the present," Clint said as he saw the boy shaking his head to signify he'd seen nothing suspicious.

Johnnie was a stocky lad, with sandy-colored hair and broad shoulders. Clint had taken an instant liking to him. He could remember when he was that age, seventeen, eighteen, and was already his own man. It looked to him as though John Denzel was well on his way to being just that.

"Tired, Johnnie?" Maggie asked.

"Reckon I'll ride over to Joyner's," the boy said. "See if Billy's about." And then he added after a short pause. " 'Course, 'less you be needin' me."

Maggie turned to Clint. "I can't think of anything, but . . ."

"See you later, Mister," Clint said with a grin. "We've counted stock and checked the feed and the fences. Not much else we can do except be ready for anything."

They watched him ride away, his spirit obviously lifted.

"He is actually going to see Billy Joyner's sister, Janey," Maggie said.

"I figured it was something like that; wanting to see his girl. What would you like to do, Miss?"

"I'd like to see you, Mister."

They had found exactly the right place for their need. Shaded, yet with dappled sunlight teasing through the grove of creek alders, the place seemed to be held by the listening light, and as though guarded from intruders.

They had taken their time. He began undressing her as they still stood with the sunlight sprinkling on them. And he had her firm, upright breasts in his hands, springy with the nipples hard and eager for his touch. She had melted into his arms. Now, with one free hand he swiftly rid himself of all clothing. And at last they stood there, totally naked, with his erection thrust between her straddling legs, his hands on her undulating buttocks, while her palms ran softly up and down his back. And their lips, their mouths met hungrily.

Then they were down on the blanket they'd brought, their bodies joined, legs and arms wrapped around each other, hardly knowing whose was which—and not caring. Caring only for the mad, driving joy that was sweeping them both into the great ocean of blending as he entered her.

Rising a little on his knees he thrust (though not too hard) his throbbing organ, and thrust again as her fist held it, stroking it as come lubricated the momentum. And then he was inside.

She was marvelously tight and wet, allowing the most joyous entry. He had no time to think or reflect on the beauty of her body, for it was all in his blood, his breath, his semen, as it came spurting into her while they pumped faster and deeper and higher.

"Oh my God, you're drowning me!" she cried, hardly able to say the words while her cry of ecstasy was more breath than vocal. And at last together coming deliriously with total abandon and for each a joy that was almost a silent scream.

Now they lay together, still entwined. He, returning more swiftly to the world, again took in his surroundings, again aware of where they were, not only in that country, but in life itself, once again knowing who he was.

For Maggie the return was slower, though no less exquisite. Until now they were again Clint and Maggie, separate though not separated.

"Thank you . . . thank you," she whispered. And with her fingers she touched the side of his face as he looked down at her.

"And I thank you," he said. He had raised up on an elbow and was looking down at her. "You are beautiful. I don't know which part of you is the most beautiful."

She blew a breath at him then, smiling with pleasure. "And you are—handsome! Yes, that's the word. Handsome. And—and I . . . I loved it . . ." And suddenly her cheeks colored, and she was embarrassed and started to laugh a little.

He found her a total delight.

And he told her so as he began caressing her and shortly mounted her again.

This time he rode very slowly, bringing his member almost all the way out and then sliding in deep, and high, and with total rigidity until he touched bottom with the head of his driving stick; moving round now, circling his hips as he held the head of his cock tight up against the wall of her vagina.

Until she was squealing and he could feel the sweat on her face and on her arms, as he held her pumping buttocks, one in each palm. Now he had her almost all the way up on her shoulders with her heels kicking him in the back, as she rode on the end of his swollen organ which he held firm as a staff right up inside her all the whole way . . . to forever . . . as they came and came again.

They rested, dozing, not falling asleep for neither wanted to let go of the presence of the other. And so they lay there, still embracing, each holding the other's hand, with the free arm enfolding the body of the other who had given such great pleasure.

Presently they disentangled and quickly dressed. Clint checked his horse's saddle, then took a look at hers. "I thought your cinch looked a mite loose there," he said. "D'you mind?" And he pulled on the cinch strap while the chestnut swelled his belly. When he'd let go again, Clint brought it up a notch. "You could ride easier like that," he said. "And safer."

"Thank you, sir."

She wasn't even listening to him, but had her eyes on his movement as he walked toward her. Instantly they were embracing.

"I'd love to do it all over again," she said.

"So would I."

"Maybe tonight—I mean if you feel like it."

He looked down at her as she stood there, some inches shorter. "I'll look forward to it," he said with a smile.

When she was mounted, and he was up on Duke, she said, "It's the best thing there is, I believe."

"What?" he asked, feigning innocence.

"Having it." And she smiled at him as though he was a backward child.

"I know," he said with a grave look on his face. "I know. Fact, there's only one thing better, I reckon."

"Why, what's that?"

"Having it again."

Her laughter was like little falling crystals as she kneed the chestnut into a walk.

They walked their horses for several yards, while Clint studied the land ahead and around them.

"I'm looking forward to some coffee," Maggie said. "I bet you are too."

Suddenly he let out a whoop and snapped the ends of his reins on the chestnut's rump as Duke broke right into a gallop.

"Cut for it! For that butte yonder!"

As the crack of the rifle split the still air and he saw the telltale puff of smoke in the rocks far away.

But there was no more firing as they sped to safety. They didn't speak but rode straight to the Bar Z. It was only when they stripped their horses that they turned to each other.

"How did you know that shot was coming?" she asked, her surprise all over her face.

"Saw the sun flashing on his barrel," Clint explained.

She was breathing heavily, her bosom revealing the fact and also the way her words came out tightly.

"I guess I've got a lot to learn."

"Yup. You do. About this here country. But on the other hand . . ."

"On the other hand—what?"

"About making love I don't believe you need to learn anything, Miss Denzel."

She was flushing then as she turned toward her horse, but he could see how it pleased her.

"I will bear that in mind, Mister Adams."

"Why the mister?" he asked in mock surprise.

"Because—or using western talk I should say 'on account of'—you called me 'Miss' . . . back there . . . a piece." And she made a very funny face and stuck out her tongue at him and said, "Yonder . . ."

It had been a disappointment to Hannibal Stringer when, his son Cyrus having informed him that "the man from the railroad" had just driven up in a spring wagon, he discovered that it was not so. In fact, for a minute it was alarming to see that his visitor was none other than Ham Rhodes, owner and boss of the neighboring HR outfit, the biggest ranch in that part of the territory.

"I want to talk to you, Stringer." The tall, raw-boned, rawhide gent got down carefully from the wagon, handing the lines to his companion—a cow-poke unknown to Hannibal Stringer. H.R. had busted his leg a while back when a yearling bronc he'd been topping-out fell on him. But the break had slowed the big man only slightly. He still couldn't ride a saddle, but he got about real quick in that gig. As old Hannibal had more often than not told his boys, "That sonofabitch gets about more places and quickern' a cat covering shit on a stone floor!"

But now Hannibal said carefully, "What about? I figgered we done all the chinnin' when I seed ya over to Wingtree." Careful, his tone, his words, but Ham Rhodes heard the whine in it.

H.R. took a minute to cuss his sore leg as he tested it on the hardpan just outside the Stringer cabin. At the same time, he was squinting at the layout, which he knew by heart anyway, checking the blue roan, the buckskin and the blaze-faced sorrel in the round horse corral; wondering if that blaze was real, or a paint job.

The old buzzard didn't miss a thing, Stringer was thinking. Damn his eyes! Man couldn't scratch his own ass 'thout that one-eyed sonofabitch knowin'.

H.R. had lost his left eye, the one that didn't squint, in a fracas up in Three Corners when fresh from jolly folly with Liz, his favorite at Helen's Place, he had received a splinter right in his orb when a gratuitous bullet, fired by a frolicking cow waddie figuring to tree the town with his heavily-liquored friends, hit a doorjam. They had been Texans and had instantly ridden off, having, so they seemed to feel, obtained their objective. It had taken a mended H.R. a goodly while to locate the prankster, and he lost no time or effort in this pursuit; the Texan paying his debt in full and contributing for the matter of that—as folks told it—to the meagre topsoil of Three Corners and environs.

"Could use some arbuckle, Stringer, an' we can jaw a bit."

That was better. The old man bent forward, turning just slightly as he placed his thumb alongside one nostril and blew, then, with his middle finger let fly from the other.

"Reckon we got somethin' left that won't strip yer guts."

Inside the cabin, which the boys had left the moment they'd seen who the visitor was, Hannibal dug up a couple of mugs, wiped one of them clean with a swift stroke of a filthy hand and set it on the table in front of his visitor. His own mug he neglected to wipe clean, even though it had been lying upside down on the dirt floor.

"I'm gonna be making a drive to the mountain come another two weeks," H.R. said. "I'll maybe need a couple of hands."

Hannibal Stringer regarded this piece of information with pursed lips, meaning he was thinking. "How many head?"

"Two, three hundred give or take."

"You expectin' trouble are ye?"

"Nothin' I can't handle. Exceptin' I want to be sure if there is trouble, it don't monument into somethin' bigger. You get me?"

"I do."

"I am thinking of Cal Owens."

"Likewise," said Stringer with a brisk nod. And then he cackled suddenly. "Them fellers on the North Fork they never do learn."

"Owens and them others will learn if they mess with my beef," H.R. said, reaching for his mug of coffee. "Jesus! Tastes like boiled piss! You tryin' to get rid of me, Stringer!"

"Why not! Why no! Such a thought never come into my head!" the old boy protested, and he blinked his eyes rapidly at his visitor to emphasize his complete innocence. "You want me to rustle you some other?"

"Never mind," growled Rhodes. "I have drunk as bad on the trail. And I ain't dead yet—I mean from drinkin' a neighbor's arbuckle. This here puts me in mind of the Injun River whiskey, by God!" He reached to his pocket and took out a cigar, not offering one to his host, though Hannibal had fastened his eyes on the rancher's shirt pocket from where at least two more cigars protruded.

Hannibal didn't especially want a smoke just then, but he said, "Could use one of them myself, now that you put me in mind of it."

With obvious reluctance the rancher handed him a cigar. "It's shipped in from Denver. Special. Don't know it you'll cotton to it. Real Havana tobacco there."

Hannibal Stringer grinned from the bottom of his heart at the reluctance with which Rhodes had given him the cigar. He bit off the bullet at the end, struck a lucifer on the bottom of his thigh, and lighted.

"I said I need a couple of good men, Stringer."

"That enough?"

"Huh." H.R. reflected. "Huh," he said again. "Make it three. Yeah, three. See if you got more; no, three'd do 'er."

"Good enough. How about hosses?"

"The HR rides the best horseflesh in the country."

Old man Stringer let out another cackle at that. "Long as a man don't look too close."

"That'll be enough of that!" Ham Rhodes was suddenly hard as a singletree. "You keep shut of that kind of talk, Stringer. You mind me!"

The old man was still chortling into his mug, his mustache and beard wet with coffee and maybe some of the contents of his nose. But his old eyes were dancing. There was nothing Hannibal Stringer liked better than action, excitement, and the game of backwatering someone or getting away with something outrageous. Like the Piller horse herd which himself and the boys had wrangled right out from under the whole of the Logan outfit over by Tensleep. Slick as a whistle. Not a hitch.

"I will be needing some new horseflesh," H.R. suddenly said, "even so." And Stringer gave a jump.

Hell, it was like that old devil had been reading his mind, coming up with reference to the stolen herd.

"The boys is still workin' on the brands," Hannibal said. "But I reckon they can find something for yeh."

"I want the best. And what about the markings?"

"Workin' on that too. It takes time, that does. Can't do a sloppy job, and then I got to keep track of the different ones. Like—hell, I just caught it in time—one of them knotheads I hired from down by Gebo changed a bay's stockings just almost exactly like the hoss had already had 'em before. Near got us a peck of trouble, he did. The damn fool! What I am sayin' is I got to be special careful not to make no mistakes. And not me—but them! Them ones I got workin' for me."

"I know that." Ham Rhodes nodded quickly. "I

know that. You have told me that about a hundred times already."

"So then maybe by now you got it in the right place in your thinkin' when you come askin' me for hosses, and there is the bizness of money. Money, Mister H. Rhodes. Me an' my boys, we don't work for sweet charity. Oh no sirreee!" And he broke off into a shrill cackling which turned into laughter: slapping his thigh, bending over, whistling, finally gasping for breath as he wheezed and grunted and groaned and sighed and finally subsided, exhausted, into his chair.

But this time he did not reach for his mug of coffee; he leaned under the table and brought up the bottle that he had stashed on the floor when he'd first heard he had a visitor.

"I'll join you on that, Hannibal," H.R. said, regaining his position. "Make it a stiff one. I got more news for you than just horseflesh."

FOUR

The Gunsmith had taken his time riding back to the spot from where that shot had come. He had realized it had to be simply a warning shot, something to haze him—and the girl too?—away from something. Some special area? They had been riding on Bar Z range, though close to the Rhodes outfit, Maggie had told him. And she had assured him that they were still very much on Bar Z ground. It occurred to Clint that the shot had just been in the way of a general hazing. A warning to not mess in anyone else's business. Maybe a warning to pull out of the country?

And he all at once wondered since it was from the Rhodes range—or appeared to be—whether Rhodes was in with with the Stringer boys and their notorious father.

Maggie had said she thought not. Then too, just because the shot came from HR country didn't mean it had to be from Rhodes. It could even be some saddle bum riding through, maybe hired for the job, and he'd maybe already ridden on, plumb out of the country.

The shot had come from a stand of timber and it was about straight-up noontime when Clint reached the thick growth of pine and spruce. From his saddle he soon picked up the hoof marks in the soft mat of mold under the trees. He dismounted and studied the tracks closely. The man with the gun had made no effort to conceal his presence. Clint read the hoof sign as having been made the day before, just about the time the shot had come while he and Maggie had been walking their horses far down the long slope that cut away from the edge of the trees. Clearly the hoof marks had been made in the late afternoon when the sun had passed far enough to the west so that the slope had been in shadow; thus the prints were still fresh and not dried out.

Clint followed the sign as it took him upward and toward the east. It led him into a game trail through the tall timber and across a small meadow, then into the timber again, winding higher and higher until he broke out into open country, high up on the rimrocks overlooking the great valley with the thin ribbon of river far below. The snow that stayed in this high country all summer long was dazzling his eyes as he surveyed the vast Panorama sweeping into the horizon.

And there, suddenly he saw the sheep. Was it the same one as before? The great, noble head, the tremendous horns curled backwards to the great shoulders and neck, and the incredible stillness.

But then, below the sheep, far below, he saw the rider picking his way carefully down a thin trail with his pony placing his feet with great care. Was it him? He felt pretty sure about it as he nudged Duke with his knees. Looking back just once he saw that the Rocky

Mountain Sheep was still there, looking off into the great sky.

"You gonna tell us what the man said, Paw?" Pierce Stringer threw his angry glance at his father who had returned from seeing Ham Rhodes depart in his gig, but had sat down, poured himself a very big drink from the almost empty bottle, and had said nothing.

At the moment Pierce asked his pregnant question, Hannibal the patriarch (as he saw himself) was swallowing his much needed refreshment in a single gulp. Leaning back, blowing a great cloud of whisky fumes into the already dense atmosphere of the cabin, he then belched, patted and rubbed his tummy, and then scratched himself vigorously in the crotch.

"Could use me somethin', by damn," he said by way of response to his son's question.

"Paw, that ain't what Pierce be askin' ya," put in Cyrus. "He is askin' about that man Road."

"Rhode*s*," Pierce said quickly, correcting his brother. "That rich bastard with all them cows an' hosses, and everythin' else a man needs in this here world, but which us poor hardworkin' Stringers ain't got hardly anythin' of."

"You can bet on that," agreed their father. "That is why I am workin' myself to the bone tryin' to support an' feed you no-good litter of dumb-ass pups! Not a one of you worth a fart in a stampede! I do all the work, all the thinking. I even got to scratch for you!" He chuckled, scratching deep into his right buttock. Then spat vigorously as a mangy, chewed-up shepherd dog limped into the room. Half his tail was gone and he had lost a lot of hair, plus one eye, courtesy of an encounter with an angry bear.

The old man never got tired of telling him he got off lucky.

"You got off lucky," he said now, true to form. "An' what the hell you doin' in the house! Who let you in!"

"I did, Paw. He didn't look so good. I thought . . ." Matt Stringer stopped as his father wheeled on him.

" 'Course he don't look good, you dumbbell; sonofabitch's got only the one eye, fer Chrissake!" And he broke into guffaws of laughter at his joke.

Suddenly he stopped. "Tend to business now, and set."

All pulled up chairs and sat around the battered table, which was marked with burns and knife cuts and even some carved initials that no one recognized. "L W loves E S" was the largest and deepest carving.

"Rhodes, he needs couple, three hands, for his drive to summer range." He dropped one heavy lid, with his other eye wide open. "Now then somethin' else. I spoke with that feller. Like I told ya, he wasn't the railroad hisself exactly, but he was doin' things with them and the bank. He was speaking in a way for the railroad, and like for the bank, which was workin' together on buying up land."

"Why buy land?" Pierce asked. "Shit, the bank's got all the land tied up with everybody owin' them, seems like."

"Shut up an' listen, boy!" Hannibal glared now at his son Harvey. "I am tellin' you how it was since one of you knotheads ast!" He sniffed, pursed his lips and a gleam entered his milky eyes. "Railroad comes through here land is gonna go way, way up, up, an' up!" He raised his palm over his head, lifting it with each word.

"You mean, you gonna sell this place, Paw?" Pierce asked. And Matt stared at his father incredulously.

"Mebbe, mebbe," said the old man.

"But what did you tell the feller?"

"Told him I'd con-sidder it!" He chuckled. "That's the way to do 'er. Said I'd give it some thought. Keep him wonderin'. See, like that. That's the way to deal with that kind. All of 'em greedy as fleas on a warthog's balls. Shit!"

"But if you sell this place, where'll we go then?" asked Harvey. "Seems to me we got a good setup here so why leave it."

"Nobody said we was goin' to leave it," his father answered. "I tolt you I told the man I'd think it over. Gives me time to make a plan."

"A plan!"

Hannibal grinned. He had caught them. He had them in his hand, right where he mostly had them anyway, but he always enjoyed playing them. Leading them this way, that; and then doubling back like and then—snap! And his idea was clear as spring water. Right here! He loved it. Working them like that! By God, a man knew where he was at when it was like that!

"Now listen . . . this feller, he wants land. But he don't want it to look like that to everybody, like him and his company is fixing to buy up everything between here and Wormsville, and from the Busted Buttes all the way to Two-Hoss River."

"Holy Moses," said Matt Stringer, lifting his forehead into a mass of wrinkles. "See what you mean there, Paw. They'd suspicion him right off on that one."

"Smart boy. So we will buy it up for him. Like we just want to get more range for our beeves. See, we're native here. Right? Then they won't suspicion it so easy. Hell, you know nobody wants the fuckin' railroad comin' through here, an' I mean *nobody!*"

"But Paw," Cyrus asked, "suppose they take it like Denzel took it when you tried buyin' him out? Hell, we can't go 'round doin' . . ."

"Shut your mouth, boy! We didn't 'go round doin' nothin'! And don't you never forget that!" He glared at his youngest.

"I ain't sayin' nothin' exceptin' to us, Paw."

"Don't be sayin' to even us, you damn fool! Not even to the Lord Hisself! You hear me now!"

An iron silence fell on the group.

At length Pierce said, "Looks to be a good plan, Paw."

"It's a damn good plan! Don't gimme that 'looks to be' shit!"

"We'll be able to name our own price!" Matt Stringer suddenly declared, his voice racing with victory. "By damn!"

"By damn," repeated his father. "We'll shove that goddam Rhodes an' his HR right the hell outta this here country."

"Or bury him—one!" said Harvey.

Their sire was chortling. "We'll drink to it, boys. We'll drink to it and be damned to any sonofabitch tries to stand in our way!"

He leaned to one side suddenly. They all knew the stance, and the gestures of face and hands that accompanied it.

Silence.

"Just remember one thing. One!" The finger stabbed
the air like a sword. "One of you fucks up, lets the cat
out, blabs, I'll personally cut his balls off!" He glared
at them. "This is the one that sets us up. But it has
got to go smooth. We got to grease it all the way.
And there will be not a one of you even farts 'thout
askin' me *first*!"

And a cackle rose in his throat, his old eyes bright-
ened and he wagged his head. And the boys picked it
up, and then they were all chortling and chuckling,
then laughing and guffawing, and drinking and even
dancing around the cabin.

In a while they grew tired. They sat down. One of
them fell, for they had all downed plenty of booze.
And at last snores began to tear into the stale air of
the tight cabin.

And old Hannibal sat in his chair, which had no
back and so he was leaning against the log wall, the
almost empty bottle loose in his hands, which were
hanging down between his legs as he continued to sit
there with his tongue sticking out, trying to touch its
tip to the end of his nose, and grinning.

Ham Rhodes stood at the window in his office in the
main house at the big HR ranch and listened to the
report from his foreman, Ty Schwinneger.

"We'll be ready to move 'em to the mountain whenever you give the sign," Schwinneger was saying. "We
might be short of hands, but with the extra you say you
can rustle up we'll handle 'er."

"You're ready now, are you. I mean right now!"

The foreman bent his bullet head and sucked his
teeth.

"What we putting up there?"

"Close on three hundred head, young stuff mostly, but all of it in good shape. They bin feeding on that good bunch grass north of Dancing Creek. Like you know," Schwinneger added.

The foreman, a short, stocky man with a broken nose and a cauliflower ear gave sign of a short foray into the professional prize ring. He had not met with much success, a fact to which his nose and one thick ear bore testimony. Yet these "decorations" added lustre to his reputation as a man handy, and sometimes even lethal with his fists, his elbows, and knees and feet, too. All to the good was how Ty Schwinneger saw it; keep the boys in line.

And it was also how his employer viewed the situation. Ty was a good hand, with the stock as well as with the men. And he was loyal. That was a big point these days, Ham Rhodes was reflecting as he sniffed and sized up the short, knotty, square-shouldered, and iron-willed bantam who could cut a man to size with a look, and did.

"I figger you got somethin' else there," Ty Schwinneger was saying. "It ain't my business, but if it's got to do with the drive up Peaceable Mountain well I . . ."

"I do." The words came crisp from the boss of the HR brand. "I got a feeling in my bones; can't put my finger on it, howsomever. It is there. Bin there this past day or two. Yup. Since we run in that hoss herd and began sacking them young broomtails."

"You figurin' with the outfit being with no hands for that time . . . somethin' like that?"

"Dunno."

"Like somebody might take a notion . . ." Ty pursued it softly, packing his chew into his cheek so that it made a bulge and he could speak more clearly around the baccy instead of trying to speak through it.

Studying his foreman as he studied the situation, Ham Rhodes at the same time heard his own thoughts asking if a man could chew tobacco and think at the same time. And the answer came—why the hell not! On this reflection he reached to his pocket for a cigar, bit off the end, licked it by rolling it between his lips, then lifting his game leg drew a lucifer sharp against his California pants. Flame burst into the room and he raised it to the cigar and drew. That was more like it, by God! A good cigar . . . like a good woman. A man needed such things. But he brought his thoughts quickly back to the situation at hand.

"You got my thought," H.R. said.

"But you was getting extra hands from Stringer. Said he'd help out, you told me."

"I'd ruther of got help somewheres else."

"Got any thoughts on it?" Schwinneger asked.

"Fact, I was just wonderin' if it might be a good notion to like go along with it."

The foreman's fierce eyebrows lifted, his mouth tightened, and something rattled in his throat, like he'd swallowed some tobacco, his boss was thinking. But Ty Schwinneger was quick.

"Hunh," he said. "You got a short nub on somethin' there, and I wouldn't argue it. Though I got to say I ain't dead sure. But I get your drift."

The boss of the HR was looking at his foreman with his good eye very wide. It was a dark eye, and now it seemed to Ty Schwinneger that it was hard as a stone; but then, as he took a second look, he felt the eye grow softer, clearing as though with a new and useful thought.

"Where will you want me to be?" Schwinneger asked.

"You tell me," H.R. said lifting the cigar slowly to his mouth, his lone eye fully on his foreman.

"With the herd."

Ham Rhodes didn't say anything. He drew on his cigar, with his eye still clamped onto the other man.

"With—here at the outfit," Ty said, feeling uncertain and wondering what his boss was up to. He'd seen Rhodes like this on some rare occasions and he wasn't enjoying himself any more than he had back then.

A lengthy silence fell while the rancher enjoyed his cigar, without taking his look off his foreman.

Finally, Schwinneger couldn't handle it any longer. "Hell, I sure as hell can't be in two places at once!"

And then for a paralyzing moment he thought his boss still wasn't going to answer. But suddenly H.R. whipped the cigar out of his mouth.

"Yes you can," he said. "And that's where you're gonna be."

"Jesus . . ." The word came more as breath than actual vocabulary.

"And so am I," H.R. said with a tight smile. "That sonofabitch Stringer is trying to diddle mc and I am going to break his goddam balls!"

"Jesus . . ." The repetition, from Ty Schwinneger's fallen mouth sounded now almost like a prayer of some kind. Maybe a prayer for deliverance from his employer's insanity. Schwinneger, least of all, could have said.

Suddenly there came a knock at the door.

"Come!" H.R. snapped out the word as he turned
to face the man who opened the door and stood on
the sill, his hat in his hand.

"Rider coming in, Mister Rhodes. Looks like that
feller what's been hangin' around the Bar Z."

"I have bin expectin' him," H.R. said. "Tell the
boys to stay on him. But don't brace him."

The door closed and H.R. turned back to his foreman. "You understand, Schwinneger? You and me
both have got to be in two places at once." His face
hardened as the foreman started to speak. "Shut up
and listen. 'Course we can't,'course it ain't possible.
But we are gonna do it. We'll do 'er!"

"But how!" The words exploded out of the foreman's intensity as he took a step forward and waved
an arm in the air, cutting it down like a scythe. "I know
we oughtta, we gotta be like that, watching both here
and the herd at the same time, but it ain't possible. It
just can't be done!"

"That is right, Schwinneger. It can't be done. But
it can be suggested."

"Hunh!" The foreman seemed to recoil at this star-
tling statement, almost as though he'd been struck.
His mouth opened, but he said nothing.

"We will deal," H.R. explained in a tone of voice
that did not offer a great deal of patience. "We will
make it like we are in both places."

"But hown' hell you gonna do that!" the practical
foreman insisted.

"Not 'you,' Mister; 'we.' How in hell are we gonna
do it!" H.R's grin was wolf-like. "We are going to fix
that Stringer's ass, but good!" He looked carefully at
the ash of his cigar before flicking it in the direction
of a plate that served as ashtray. "We will simply let

them think we are in one place when we are in the other. And like that. Here? No, not here but there! Get it?"

"But how?" Schwinneger's eyes were almost popping with his frustration at trying to understand his employer. He always hated it when H.R. was like this—dumb, downright stupid, a wall of deaf-and-dumb where a man couldn't understand a damn thing what he was sayin'. Why couldn't he talk simple, clear and plain! Like any sensible cowman!

"Hmm . . ." The boss of the HR brand stood stolidly in front of his impatient foreman, as though the nearly violent man in front of him had simply asked him the time of day, or what the weather was outside, or about the feed up on the high range. "Hmm. Hunh." As he took a very slow drag on his cigar, his one eye was thoughtful, figuring a way to make what he wanted to say sound simple.

"By the simplest trick in the world, my lad."

"How's that?"

"By telling them." H.R. opened his hands, sweeping the room with the smoke of his cigar and grinned wolfishly at his foreman.

"Telling them! What you mean—telling them! Telling them what?"

Ham Rhodes's dry chuckle fell in to the room. The expression on his foreman's face was really rich.

"Why telling them I'm with the herd, and then me or somebody telling them no, you are; like letting them know, without actually saying it too clear. Then showing up at the outfit. Here. Then switching it around again and showing up at the herd. You get it?"

Ty Schwinneger looked as though he had been garrotted. His dark face had turned several shades

darker, indeed it was almost scarlet, and for a moment
his boss thought he was going to have a fit.

But a man had to be careful how he spoke to Ham
Rhodes and fortunately Ty remembered this; indeed,
it had always come as second nature to him, having
learned like so many others, the hard way.

At last the foreman gave up. "I dunno." He wagged
his head, and H.R. thought he saw a little sweat flying
about as Schwinneger slapped his hands against his
legs, then opened his arms as though ready for the
scaffold at last.

His employer watched him with not well-concealed
glee. Ty was a good man, no question about that, but he
did need taking down a notch now and again. Bugger
would else get the bit in his teeth and be all over the
place. It was a good moment, and a good way to rein
him in.

"Ever watch a slick diceman switching tops and
flats?" H.R. asked in a very quiet voice.

Ty simply continued to stare.

"Hard to see him. Fact, it mostly ain't possible.
You know why?"

"Got fast hands, I reckon," Ty said reasonably.

"Trick is he directs your attention to something else.
One reason a feller like that usually talks a helluva lot.
Gets you looking elsewhere, and thinking maybe of
something else, an'—pow! He's switched 'em, and
nobody's the wiser."

For a moment Ty Schwinneger continued to look
nonplussed. Then abruptly his face cleared. "You
figger you can pull something like that on old man
Stringer and his boys? Well—maybe on them boys—
but that old man, he is slick as a whistle, that old boy.
A slicker."

H.R. was nodding. "That's what I know," he said. "That's what I know. But see, you watch him and you begin to notice he's a man thinks he knows everything. He figgers himself—just like you say— too slick to be took by anyone. Especially a simple old rancher man and his foreman who all they know about is cattle and stuff. You getting my point, Ty?"

"I am. I am." Ty was first of all impressed by the way H.R. had spoken to him. It was rare, the boss almost never called him 'Ty.' He was impressed and felt the moment of their relationship strongly. He knew too that the herd was everything to Ham Rhodes. The herd and the ranch. Hell, the man had worked for it and he'd earned it. And here—and here, by God, there was something different in the man standing before him. He wasn't sure just what it was, but it was there.

"I am with it," Ty Schwinneger said, suddenly feeling his place as foreman of the HR in a different way. Not that he could ever have said what it was exactly, but it was there. By God, he was thinking, that old buzzard has changed or somethin' or maybe he is getting old. Damn! Next thing you knew he'd be offering one of them expensive, special sent cigars.

"We'll work on it," H.R. was saying. "For now, that's about it. We got to get our hands on some men. And the fact that those extra men will be from Stringer can help us."

"How so?"

"On account of everything we say or do will get back to that old bastard pronto. Thought you would have picked up on that long about now. Come on.

You got to be sharper than that. On account of this
here has got to work. And by God, it is going to
work or my name ain't Ham Rhodes." He nodded in
agreement with his own declaration.

"I got it good now," Ty said, and he felt good
again.

H.R's cigar had gone out and now Ty Schwinneger
watched him take a lucifer from his shirt pocket and
strike it on his thumbnail one-handed. The rancher's
dead eye shone as he bent slightly to the flame. Then,
blowing out a cloud of smoke he turned his good eye
solemnly on his foreman.

"Schwinneger, you look like you could use a good
cigar." And H.R. reached to his pocket and pulled out
a well-built panatela.

Ty Schwinneger was silent as he accepted the cigar,
bit off the little bullet at the end, and lit up. He didn't
know what he was feeling, but he fully realized the
importance of the moment. Well, a man couldn't never
let himself take it easy and slow and figure he knew
what was going to happen next. Because you never
knew. One cigar in a dozen years. That was for sure
something bigger than a small thing.

He looked over at his employer as he drew on the
panatela. H.R. was scratching inside his ear with the
clean end of the dead wooden match.

He sat easy on Duke, a quirly hanging from his lip,
as from the rim of the long, dish-shaped coulee he
surveyed the approach to the HR ranch. It was no
small outfit. He'd realized that earlier as he'd ridden
in from the south, passing HR stock, checking for
any Bar Z stuff mixed in with the Rhodes brand.
And finding some. He also spotted a few re-worked

brands; running-iron work done by somebody who evidently knew his business. Only the Gunsmith had a sharp eye; an eye, that when he looked at a thing, he saw it.

He hadn't been challenged by any outriders, though he'd seen them scattered along his route. They'd picked him up soon after he'd left the Denzel spread and had watched all the way.

Good. It was what he'd expected and wanted. His plan depended on their knowing he was about, and intending to ride in.

For he'd gotten the definite feeling that Ham Rhodes was a man he had to face head-on, and right now. A tough old boy, Maggie and her brother had told him. Tough as a raw bronc, and just as ornery. But for himself, the Gunsmith definitely felt Ham Rhodes to be a man with corners, a man you could confront, not a snake. At the same time, he had a very strong notion that there was a snake somewhere about in the present mess in Wingtree and the surrounding country.

Yes, there was a horsebacker yonder, and he looked to be the same one he'd spotted more than an hour ago down by the little creek with all the willows.

Well, Rhodes, he could see, sure kept a tight nub on his men. He wondered if it had been Rhodes who'd written the warning at the hanging tree he'd come on just a few days back. And it surprised him how it seemed all that long ago when it wasn't even a week that had gone by since he'd ridden in on that corpse and its buzzards.

Now he kicked Duke into a walk down the coulee, quartering easy-like, with his attention taking in everything from the distant horizon to the whole periphery

that was available to his sweeping vision. The sun
was real hot on the backs of his hands. Unlike a lot
of cowhands Clint Adams didn't like wearing gloves
too much. Only when he was roping, actually, and
then it was necessary. But he'd known old men with
palms like leather, and knuckles like they were knots
cut out of a tree, men whose hands seemed to have
existed before they, themselves had come along to fit
onto them so that they could work. He favored that
kind of men; they did their day's work and didn't
complain, and by the time they got old enough to
tell the next weather in their bones, the younger ones
such as himself could read their sign and figure which
way the trail was to go. They were the silent ones, the
ones who really worked the frontier and marked out
the West.

Suddenly, without any warning Duke shied. In the
same instant the Gunsmith had drawn his handgun
and shot the head off the rattlesnake.

While through his binoculars, Ham Rhodes, standing in the window of his office in the big log ranch
house, muttered an admiring curse. The word was
said neither in devotion nor irritation but rather as an
acknowledgement of what he described to himself as
'pretty damn fancy shooting.'

He was glad he had seen it. He had a better notion
now of the kind of man he was up against.

"Is it him?" Ty Schwinneger asked his boss's back.

"It ain't Robert E. Lee." H.R. lowered the glasses
and turned back into the room. "I just seen him shoot
that rattler what spooked his horse quickern' a goosed
bronc sunfishin'." He wagged his head, laying the
glasses carefully on the desk. "Well, we will see what
this Mister Gunsmith feller's up to."

"He is up to stickin' his goddam nose into our business it begins to look like to me," said Schwinneger sourly.

"Mebbe. Exceptin' it ain't his nose you got to watch out for, it's that gun of his. I can see why he has got that moniker, by golly. Gunsmith. Hunh . . . That's a good one. That's a real good one."

His foreman simply stood there, swing-hipped, his thumbs hooked into his aged belt, feeling the gap in his back teeth with his tongue where, the day before, Cookie, the outfit's "doctor-dentist" had removed the blistering toothache that had been bothering his old sidekick for "too damn long enough."

Ty Schwinneger now smiled, carefully, his face feeling that whole lot different the way it does when pain is removed.

"The boys are ready," he said again, more to himself in reflection this time.

"They better be," muttered H.R. "He don't look like a man to mess with. How many you got?"

"Four. I'll have my eye on it."

"You got Simes there. That feller with the big nose."

"Simes is there. I told him to handle the gabbin'."

"Good enough," H.R. said. "We'll just see how he handles himself, 'fore we get closer. Hell, Simes and the boys might settle the whole thing right now. Then we'll know where we're at."

"With that feller?"

"I wasn't talkin' about George Washington."

Ty Schwinneger grinned. He rubbed his nose with the back of his hand. "I done it like you tolt. I didn't tell them any setup exceptin' to haze him off."

"That's right. Don't tell 'em anything."

"But how come? If that Gunsmith feller's fast as everyone let's on, and he sure handled that rattler real neat, then they be wanting some kind of advantage."

"I want to see how Simes and his three buddies handle it." Rhodes said softly, his eyes thoughtful. "We have got a big tussle comin' up, my lad, and I want men what can handle theirselves."

"But those boys used to be with Stringer," Ty insisted. "They have got to be tough."

H.R. took a drag on his cigar. "Old man Stringer is not dumb. But you look to have lost any sense you might ever have had, for Christ sake. Do you think he would've let me have them three if they'd been good enough to backwater a man like him on that black hoss?" He spat suddenly in the loose direction of the cuspidor next to his desk, his aim being true, and continued in the same tone to his foreman. "You bein' a cattleman know for Chrissake that any trail boss'll spend time shaking down his crew 'fore he gets them beeves moving."

Ty Schwinneger, caught again by the boss's cutting edge, blinked sheepishly. But he held his tongue. He had learned early never to talk back to Mr. Rhodes.

"We'll be watching," H.R. said. "From the kitchen. And you be ready. On account of I might send you out if things get hairy. I don't want him killed. But I might want him roughed up." He was looking at his foreman's cauliflower ear, as the Gunsmith rode closer. In another moment or two he would pass from view, rounding the corner of the ranch house, and so H.R. nodded to his foreman.

"We'll pick him up through the kitchen window," he said. And he turned on his good heel carefully so his game leg could avoid the corner of his big rolltop desk.

Ty Schwinneger put his hat back on his head as he followed, his tongue still playing with the gap where his angry tooth had been.

He couldn't see them, but he knew in his bones that they were watching him from the house. He kept Duke at a walk now, easy, slow but not dragging. Duke's gait was careful as his rider missed nothing from under the brim of his big Stetson hat.

He rode up the long rise of ground that paralleled the ranch house and then all at once he was in the flat area outside the horse corral and the barn, about a couple of hundred yards from a thin, winding creek lined with willow. The house was in full view now on the near side of the creek, a large and rambling building built of spruce logs that had evidently been cut on the higher ground leading up toward the rimrocks, and then snaked down with horses; for Clint spotted the narrow log trail beyond the corral.

And now he was facing the bunkhouse straight ahead, with the ranch house, a good bit bigger, and also built of logs, several yards off to his right.

He had just started to turn Duke in the direction of the big house when he saw the bunkhouse door open and a man stepped out. He was followed by three other men who quite casually spread out, for an instant appearing simply to be going about their chores. Yet the Gunsmith wasn't fooled, he had instantly spotted the weaponry at their hips, and the surly looks they threw in his direction. It was obvious that they were positioning themselves for crossfire. At the same time, he noticed movement on the far side of the corral, by the watering trough.

"I am here to see Ham Rhodes," Clint said in a voice that was unmistakable in its purpose and force. There was no doubt that all heard this declaration. And it had served to halt their movement, fixing them in their positions with his aggressive tone that had taken away their initiative.

That he was in their crossfire didn't bother the Gunsmith. He was wholly familiar with such play; understanding that they had mainly wanted him to realize their setup, he realized too that there had to be a wider coverage out of view. They would be playing for him to keep his attention only on the four who were visible.

It was the man who had led them out of the bunkhouse who now spoke.

"Mister Rhodes ain't seein' visitors this day, Mister. You can tell me your business."

"My business is with Rhodes and I am not going to say it again," Clint said. He nodded in the direction of the big house. "I'll just say one thing. You have got four guns on me, if that's what your play is, plus more by the trough and that window yonder. But you'll be first, Mister."

"Lemme take him, Simes," said a man to his left, trying to catch the Gunsmith's attention.

Simes, the man who had first spoken now reached over very slowly with his left hand and unbuckled his belt, then slowly lowered his weapon to the ground.

"You wouldn't shoot a unarmed man, now would you, Gunsmith? Boys! You boys, drop yer guns. Gunsmith, you wouldn't shoot us without we got our guns, now would ya?" Simes's voice was laced with sneer

and laughter, as he nodded to his three companions
to disarm themselves.

"Why not?" Clint said, dismounting swiftly and not
taking his eyes off the man Simes. "It makes easier
shooting; like popping dummies in a shooting gallery."
And he stood there, firm as a gun barrel while his hard,
cold words hit them.

Clint knew his men. It wouldn't be the hardness
or coldness that reached them, but the casual way
he spoke, the swift ease. But he had a lot of his
attention on the window where he had seen a shape
in the reflecting sunlight.

And he saw that the man called Simes was off-
guard. Just a flash, an instant of inattention, and at
that moment he started to walk toward the house.

In the next moment the door opened and the big man
with the cane and limp, and only one eye emerged. He
was unarmed.

"You Rhodes?" the Gunsmith asked.

"I am." Ham Rhodes stood tough as a wagon axle
right in front of his own doorway.

"Then maybe you'll tell that other feller in that
window there to come out and join us, and that one
by the trough. I've got somethin' to say to you, and
I do want some of your men to hear it."

Suddenly Ham Rhodes burst into a crash of laughter.
"By God! By God if that don't shoe the mare! Simes,
you and the boys get back to work. And Schwinneger!"
He had half turned around to the house in back of
him. "You too." He took a step forward, limping,
and held it, sniffing, with a strange grin on his face.
"Come on in. We'll set." And then his voice loud
again, he called out, "Schwinneger, tell Amy to hustle
coffee and some of them sinkers." He nodded to Clint.

"C'mon, Gunsmith, coffee's what we got and that's what we'll have. C'mon." He had turned, somewhat painfully, Clint could see, but without swearing, and now started back into the house.

"What's yer name?" he said over his shoulder, with his back to his visitor. "Yer real name."

But Clint didn't answer. Out of the side of his eye and without breaking stride or turning his head, he saw the four men pick up their gunbelts and walk away.

"Eh?" said Rhodes, still without turning to face his visitor.

And Clint still didn't answer.

Another moment or two passed while they entered H.R.'s office and the rancher turned and shut the door, pushing it to with his cane. Then he limped over to one of the two big armchairs in front of the stone fireplace and seated himself. The chairs were loosely covered with buffalo robes, and looked really comfortable to Clint, so he too sat down.

Ham Rhodes was facing him now and he looked into the man's good eye, sizing him, noting, too, the strong jaw, the stubble of beard, the firm mouth and jaw under the thick mustache, the large ears, which before he took off his big hat had been pressed down a bit by the brim.

"I ast you what yer name was, mister. You ain't Mister Gunsmith like, I am sure. Or Tom or Hank Gunsmith. What's yer name?" And he leaned forward a little, his tone neither friendly nor hostile.

"I talk to a man's face, not his back," Clint said, nor was his tone either for or against the man sitting in front of him. "I am Clint Adams. And I have come to talk about the beeves I see in your stock with Bar Z ear markings and some pretty sloppy running iron work."

"You a stock detective, Mister?"

"Nope. I am foreman for the Bar Z."

The big man's eyebrows moved up at that and he grunted. "I see. I see said the blind man an' he didn't see at all. You know that rhyme?"

"What about the Bar Z brands that have been ironed into HR, and what about the ear markings?"

"You accusing me of rustling Bar Z stuff?"

"I am not accusing you of anything. I am telling you what I have seen, and asking a question." He leaned forward, his forearms on his knees to add to what he had to say, but at that moment a woman entered carrying a tray with two steaming mugs of coffee and a plate of sourdough biscuits.

She was not young, yet she wasn't old. Clint would have said she was in her early forties. He wondered if she was Rhodes's wife, but the thought flicked through as she left the room, giving him a very brief look to size him up. Clint liked that rather. Obviously, she wasn't any cringing flower, but simply looked at him to see what he was. And as he turned back to Rhodes, he realized that the rancher had been watching him, seeing his reaction to the woman.

"I do allow that some Bar Z stock might've got mixed in with HR. Happens, as you moren' likely know." The rancher lifted his steaming mug. "About the ears, an' other markings, I got no notion. I don't steal cattle, mister. Nor hosses. And I am making that point damn clear. You understand me?"

"I do." But Clint wasn't backing an inch. "I'll be riding out there again and I could go with yourself or your ramrod and we can take another look-see."

"I will send you with Schwinneger," Rhodes said.

"He your foreman?"

The nod was slow, not very marked, but the words were firm. "He is the man I'll be sending with you, Adams."

Clint saw that this line had been pursued far enough and now he said, "Did you know Hank Denzel?"

His host nodded. "Fact is, since you be askin' about brands getting switched, Denzel was pretty handy with a runnin' iron."

"You know that for a fact?"

"Somebody was rustling HR stock, and as you surely know by now at your age—whatever that is— the nesters and all of them start their herds by branding slicks and changing brands on the big outfits' stock."

"You're saying Hank Denzel was doing that?"

The rancher squinted at him now, closing his blind eye completely, pursing his lips, then reaching up to scratch the side of his jaw and finally with his little finger he dug some wax out of his ear. "You doubtin' my word, Mister?"

"I'll let you know that after I take a look at your stock." Clint said, and he stood up.

His host now got to his feet and stood facing him. "I have heard of you, Adams. And I seen the way you handled the boys out there." He nodded toward the window. "I could use a good man."

"For what?"

"Ramrod."

"You don't like the man you've got?"

"Ty? He's a good man. I ain't aimin' to get rid of him. But I need some extra. I need a man who'll not only ramrod the boys but doesn't mind throwin' down on what's necessary."

Clint kept his eyes directly on the other man as he shook his head.

"Gun ain't for hire—that it?" H.R. sniffed and looked toward the cuspidor to aim some spittle, but then evidently decided not to, since he realized that he wasn't chewing anything anyway, and it was just habit.

Clint Adams was looking directly at him when he said, "I'll be over with somebody and we'll check for Bar Z stuff. Likely tomorrow. Your ramrod wants to come along he can find me, in a day or two." He stared to the door of the room, then stopped with his hand on the nob and turned back to his host. "It's not my gun that's not for hire, Rhodes. It's—*I* ain't for hire!"

FIVE

"Understand, my dear, that Wingtree could become like any one of the more profitable towns in the West. It's all a matter of how certain arrangements are made." It was Elijah Soames beaming the good news to his dinner companion, a blond lady of attention-catching physical dimensions, not to mention a charm and ambiance that supported her provocative bust, her haunches, the delicacy, yet firmness of her perfectly modeled hands, the creamy, statuesque neck and shoulders; but mostly the tantalizing assurance in two walnut-colored eyes. An assurance that knew sexual conquest by its first name, and handled business with a skill unequalled in her calling.

"I'm all ears, Ellie," she replied, her voice reaching his ear as though a dove had spoken. "But what about Wingtree becoming the very *best* in the West?"

His grin spread all over his chubby face. "Agreed. Bravo, my dear!" He chuckled and reached for the bottle of wine with one hand while with the other he picked up her glass.

"Yes I will, thank you," she said.

"Have you heard the latest?" He gazed at her archly, feeling the wine, eager to tell the exciting story, taking in her delicious sexuality which was almost equalled by the regality of her bearing. Yet, she couldn't have been more than in her early thirties.

"What's the latest, Ellie?"

He raised his glass and she followed suit. "Here's to fun and good times. Here's to passion."

"And money! Elijah, how gross of you to forget money, without which life would be unbearable."

He loved it when she gave him the *la-de-da* talk. And it was indeed *hoity-toity*, definitely not *hoi polloi*, he told himself. Yet he knew a bit of her background. He knew where she came from. The East. Boston. It always astonished him to realize that this beautiful, luscious creature from a New England best-family background, was living out here in the wild and woolly, and running—or until recently had run—one of the greatest sporting houses in the West. Candice Thoreau—or Candy as she was better known—was also a marvel of invention when it came to the activities of lust. In a word, he was delighted to realize that she simply drove him crazy in bed.

"So just what is the latest?" she repeated after they had downed the toast. There was a twinkle in her eye, while his eager orbs were devouring the curve of her bosom.

But he came back to his story. "It's delicious, my dear. Listen to this. You know the lady with the marvelous name—Madame Jew's Harp . . ."

"I do indeed. She is also known as The Sydney Duck."

"Ah! How's that? What's that mean? I hadn't heard

that one." And he leaned back, patting the table cloth with the palm of his pudgy hand.

"It means she's from the Australian prison camps." Candy Thoreau's smile was controlled. "But I've a notion that she has a heart of gold."

At this they both broke into laughter. Elijah sat back dabbing at his eyes with the knuckle of his forefinger, while reaching for his handkerchief.

"Well, at any rate, The Sydney Duck—what a great monicker!" he chuckled. "She was simply trying to run an honest business in Denver when one evening she got herself bitten by a charming fellow with the fascinating name of Seaborn O'Toole. And she had him arrested."

"Really!" Candy Thoreau's eyes were bright with laughter as she put down her empty glass, and Elijah reached for the bottle. "What was the charge? Animal love?"

"Well, actually, Seaborn O'Toole got out of it by simply hiding his upper plate, so that the toothmarks Madame Jew's Harp wanted to show in evidence wouldn't fit him at the trial."

At that they both laughed uproariously.

"It reminds me of the time Molly Sue Annie slickered those fat gamblers from K.C. in Deadwood," Candy said with a wicked smile.

"How was that?"

"She bet them she could take all her clothes off and walk down Main Street from the Broken Dollar to Sweeney's Place and not a man would whistle or say a damn thing."

"So did she?"

"She sure did. Their money on the barrelhead first and she made them put down a small fortune."

"And she covered them?"

"She covered with a free ride on the house for the whole bunch. There were about ten of those smart alecks in on it."

Elijah was grinning in anticipation. "And so what happened?"

"Molly Sue went back of the bar, stripped and when she came out she was packing a nice little bulldog derringer. There wasn't a snicker or a grin or even any damn thing going on except a lot of heavy breathing, let me tell you! And she took her time walking the whole distance."

At this they both collapsed into riotous laughter.

"Candy—I love ya!"

"No you don't. Don't hand me that stuff. Let's get back to business now."

"And then—after?" He cocked a thin eyebrow at her,

"Let's see where we get to."

But he caught the tease in her smile and voice. He had already locked the door, but now he got up and checked it again.

She was already taking off her clothes as he returned. The bulge in his trousers drove between her parting legs as he put his arms around her, and began pumping his erection as he felt her breath gasping against his face.

"Where do you want it, my dear? On the sofa or the floor this time."

"On the table. There. On the table . . ."

Elijah Soames awakened suddenly in surprise at finding that he had fallen asleep with Candy Thoreau's legs wrapped around his head, and his own legs wrapped around hers. Memory returned, and he recalled the tremendous excitement on the tabletop and how they had slithered to the floor to complete their passion on the buffalo rug, with himself up on his knees, and the girl on her shoulders as he drove his fierce erection into her soaking orifice, as she begged him to come, come, come. Which he did, obliging her with more come than he'd ever given her before.

"My God, my God!" she'd screamed the words into his ear, digging her fingers, her nails into his pumping buttocks, while she squirmed and bucked beneath him in a frenzy of coming.

They had rested then, locked in each other's arms and legs. Whispering, dozing, until one or the other—neither would have remembered who was the initiator—began to touch, then caress fingers along the other's still sweating body. Until she rose up on her hands and knees and fisting his rigid organ began stroking it, forehand and backhand, alternating as her fist slid on the abundance of come. And then she was down on him, taking his cock deep in her mouth, down her throat, and sucking long, luscious lickings . . . while he thought he would explode.

But he maintained, and so reaching down with his hand, he laid his palm over her bush and drew her around so that she at last lifted her leg over him, lowering her wetness into his face. He almost cried out with joy, but couldn't make a sound for his mouth was at work on her squirming vagina, licking and sucking, and nibbling at the wet, puffy lips. He knew that nothing, absolutely nothing in his whole life had ever tasted so good.

He was aware then that she was mumbling, but because his still stretching stick was in her mouth, halfway down her throat, indeed, he couldn't make out what she was saying. Then suddenly, she released him, and his cock sprang into the room as she gasped, "Come with me. For Chrissake come!"

And Elijah absolutely obliged her.

It was shortly before 10 o'clock or a warm evening in July when the stationmaster at Big Spring, Wyoming, heard sounds that brought him to the window of his little shack. He wagged his grey head and sniffed.

"Hearin' things, must be. Could've sworn I heerd hosses."

"Wouldn't surprise me," his assistant said indifferently, picking his nose. "Could be passengers for the ten o'clock."

Outside the stationmaster's shack the "passengers", who numbered five, were already dismounted and now they adjusted their masks, and marched into the station.

The stationmaster and his assistant raised their hands.

"Tie 'em," Paw Stringer said to his son Cyrus.

While the last knot was being tied, they heard a locomotive whistle moaning in the distance. With the stationmaster and his assistant immobilized, the old man and his boys scattered to strategic positions, as the train, trailing sparks from the locomotive stack, pulled to a stop.

The attack was executed with almost mechanical precision. No more than thirty seconds had passed on the old man's horologe from when the fireman and engineer were told to throw up their hands, and the moment when Harvey and Matt Stringer leaped into the express car.

"Open the safe!" Harvey snapped at the startled messenger.

"Can't! It's got one of them time locks. Can't be opened till we get to Cheyenne."

"Like hell it can't!" Harvey shouted. "Mister, you open that there safe, I mean now, or I will blow you to merry hell, and I mean right now!" He had shoved the muzzle of his gun right into the messenger's face, which had turned chalk white.

Suddenly, his twin Matt said, "He ain't lyin'." He had been examining the safe. "But lookee over yonder!"

He had nodded toward a small, heavily built box containing a number of oblong packages. Now he stepped over quickly and lifted one, swearing with delight as he felt its weight, and then whammed the package against a corner of the box. A shower of $20 gold pieces hit the floor.

"Here's what we want, by damn!" Harvey cried. "There's a goddam fortune here!"

Twenty minutes later after the coaches had been raided and the passengers relieved of all valuables, the old man and his sons withdrew. A few shots were fired to steady any thought of pursuit, though none was expected from the thoroughly chastened victims, and then the Stringer family raced for their horses.

Back home the boys counted their takings; Paw doing the division, with himself accepting the lion's share.

"Bein' as I gived the brains to the outfit, plus the muscle, and by God the whip, you rapscallions!" But he was chuckling all over his boney-whip body. "Showed 'em, by jingo! Showed the bastards!"

They were in the kitchen and now he stood suddenly

hard before his four sons. "We got one more to take on," he said amiably, taking out a fresh chew from his sagging pants pocket.

"Shit! Ain't that gonna be risky, Paw?" It was Cy speaking.

"You young whelp, you got yer balls froze up with the little excitement, have ye? Shit! By God, I don't want to hear one more of such a kind of talk from you, you little sniffer!" And he reached out suddenly and grabbed Cyrus by his shirt front. "Got a notion to whip yer ass, right now!" But he shoved his son away. "Momma boy, that's what you are. Still, I need you for the next one."

It was Pierce who felt sufficiently emboldened to ask the question that had been teasing all of them ever since Paw had announced his decision to hit the U.P. "That feller from the railroad what come. He the man layin' it out like?" The words had been put carefully, and the tone of voice too. But their curiosity was greater than their fear, at least so it was for Pierce.

"Mind yer business now, Mind!" Paw's hand suddenly whipped to an armpit to scratch furiously. "We be doing business with a certain party, not that it is business of yourn', but some of this we just counted out was for fun. It goes to the feller who come to see me that time." Swiftly he held up his hand to stem any protest. "We get a cut. Exceptin' not like so much as we thought." He held up his hand again. "It'll be sizeable. Sizeable. And don't fergit, we got the other. Same understanding. We make the haul and then we slice the cake."

"What's to stop us making our slice a bigger one," said Pierce reasonably.

"On account of that feller, he has knowledge of the shipments and where they be coming from and all like that."

"You mean he knows how much we got here?" asked a startled Harvey, looking down at the gold pieces which were reflecting in the light of their two coal oil lamps.

"That he does." The old man chuckled, scratching his crotch this time. "More or less," he added, and winked slowly over one of his prominent eyes.

"When we gonna do it, Paw?" Cyrus asked.

"Saturday night."

"Holy shit!" It was Matt who brought out the first exclamation and he was followed instantly by his brothers.

"That's crazy, Paw!"

"It's too goddam soon. We got to lay low!"

"We be askin' for big trouble being foolish like that," Pierce said, summarizing the filial devotion.

"It ain't. You knotheads! The law won't even be thinkin' anybody'd hit again so soon. They won't expect it. They'll be jiggered for a fare-thee-well, boys!" And he reached for the bottle which had been waiting unattended for too long, in the light of the surprises he was dropping on them.

Finally, they subsided into merriment and self-congratulations over what they had pulled, and were still going to pull on the U.P.; and also they could read the signs that their sire was dropping in their path, the signs which said that Mister U.P. Man was going to get it too up the old rooty-tooty.

The old man had also pointed out to his offspring the simple fact that it was just because the second hit would be so soon after the first one that no one would be expecting it. In this he had exhibited extraordinary patience, as he rarely did, but this was a moment of high import. And so he kept a check-rein on his brisk temper and explained, saying it over and over, like a litany.

By the evening that the strike was to take place the boys were in line; they were even enthusiastic. There was no other choice. Paw Stringer had all along known very well what he was up to. His first step had been to find a special location not near his ranch which would be their hideout. Naturally—he shrewdly figured—should anybody suspect the Stringer boys they would check out the outfit, but they would not be there. They would be able at any time to be well concealed in their special hideout. This base was located by the old scoundrel in a heavily wooded region of bottomland near Skyhook Pass, a thinly settled community; sheltered and protected—almost hidden in a tangle of thick brush and vines—and when the Stringers were in residence, further protected by their vicious hostility.

Briskly, the old man gave orders for resettling at the camp a night prior to the planned holdup. The raid took place at Nimbus Station, a stop for water mostly, though passengers also were allowed to board.

Following the same plan used in the Big Spring holdup, the twins confronted the engineer and fireman at gunpoint while Pierce and Cyrus leaped onto the express car.

The messenger had swung open the door of the express intending to hand over several packages to the station agent. But braced by Cyrus and Pierce he stepped quickly back inside the car, drew his gun and fired at the bandits. Pierce and Cyrus both returned the fire, then Pierce leaped into the car and slammed the barrel of his handgun against the side of the messenger's head, knocking him to the floor.

"Tell the engineer to hitch off this car!" Paw Stringer, who was standing on the roadbed alongside the engine, shouted back to one of his sons who was running along the tops of the cars. "Tell him to snake it down the line!"

Moments later, the express car began to move slowly away from the train. It stopped several hundred yards from the station.

Matt and Harvey had the front of the train covered, while now Pierce and Cyrus smashed open the safe. The boys swept $5,000 into a sack.

Minutes later Paw and his highly efficient sons were hightailing it west toward Skyhook Pass.

And that night they frolicked in celebration. As usual, the whiskey flowed, and so did the stories. The old man never tired of recounting his incredible adventures, and the boys never grew weary of listening. Indeed, they had participated in not a few of these escapades. Like the time down in the Oklahoma Territory when, chased by a goodly number of lawmen and outraged citizens, Hannibal and his boys had enlivened matters by capturing four of their pursuers, loading them to the roots of their hair with Injun River whiskey, and then turning them loose. And then to top this fabulous monkeyshines Paw had galloped into the nearby town, where the law and their citizen deputy detachment had quartered themselves, and had made off with a nifty little buckskin plus a blaze-faced roan from the livery stable. Frenzied pursuit had followed this caper, but to no avail. Paw and his chortling brood escaped plumb out of the Territory.

"We'll lay low now," Paw was saying, as he finished retelling the story of the drunken posse members and the two horses he had stolen from the livery; the buckskin belonged to a deputy marshal whom he particularly enjoyed acing. "We'll head back to the outfit."

"Paw, what we gonna do about the money?" Cyrus asked.

"Boy, you are simple, a bit like your Maw; God rest her soul. But that is a fact and for certain sure." And the old man spat indolently into the heart of a bunch of sage that had caught his eye as he reflected on his deceased spouse.

Then—" 'Course, boys, it's gettin' to be time for a little fun time."

"Hey, Paw, you mean like some of that pussy?" Cyrus asked, beaming all over from head to foot, while his brothers chortled.

"I ain't meanin' hosses," their father said astringently. "Last time I was in Sky I listened up some of them gals at Lolly's place. Told 'em to be on the ready, we might be needin' 'em. So now's the time."

"By damn! It sure is!"

So saying, the whole family let out a bunch of hoots and hollers and stomped out of the cabin, found their horses, and started off to Skyhook Pass, each one of the five with the very same thought in mind.

It was real great Paw Stringer was thinking just then, how a family could get really together on something.

The little cemetery was at the south end of the town, lying quietly on a low rise of ground edged by a grove of creek alders. Clint had ridden Duke out to the small cluster of graves with their various markings. He noted some of these in particular as he sought Hank Denzel's place. It was good to see that frontier humor had not died with the person whose last resting place it was marking. One marker in particular caught his eye. It was a wooden slab with a carving of five playing cards—all aces. Underneath was carved "The Loser." There were others, also pithy and humorous; but he didn't dally, for he soon spotted the new marker which was obviously Hank's and the flowers that he knew Maggie had left. She had described the headpiece to him, and he saw how appropriate it was. A simple block of uncarved stone. And coming closer now he read the inscription—Henry Denzel—and his dates.

Well, it was sure Hank Denzel. Stone. Solid. And honest as the mountains. That was Hank. He stood there for some while now, his hat in his hand, feeling the sun on his back, standing with his feet in the shadow thrown by Hank's stone.

When he heard Duke's bridle jangling again he looked up, realizing how long he must have been there, lost in his feeling. Tomorrow he was going to check the H.R. range for Bar Z stock. He planned to take Johnnie Denzel with him. The boy was a solid one. Maggie had also wanted to come, but he had told her she could help best by watching the outfit while they were away.

Meanwhile, he was taking this time to visit a minute or two to say so long to his friend Hank, and also to check out the local gossip. In most towns of the West— he could have said in all of them—there were certain areas where gossip and folklore, opinion and conjecture, circulated amongst those denizens who assumed a knowledge of more than met the average eye. And while much of such gossip was off the mark, the old saying that smoke pointed to fire often proved true. And of course there were certain serious areas for such exchanges—the barber, the eating place, the gambling hall, and most certainly, the saloon, dancehall, and the cribs, amongst the sporting sorority.

And so after standing there a while with whatever was left of Hank Denzel—his decaying body and the earth touching it, the memory of the times they'd spent together down on the Hoodoo Ranch on the south fork of Wood River, and in Meeteetse, and around Sunshine Basin, and a whole lot else, centering finally on just missing a good man—he decided he'd head back to town.

It wasn't far, though being a horseman all the way through he hadn't walked. Habit. A cowboy's hat and his horse took a man everywhere; sometimes even indoors. Clint chuckled at the thought, realizing that even though he was only a sometime cowhand, he still had the habit. And so he mounted Duke and rode back down the low hill and onto Main Street, walking the big black in obedience to the town law that forbade running a horse in town, looking straight ahead, but at the same time keeping a good vigilance out of the sides of his eyes. For he knew now that he'd been marked. While nothing had come from the warning shot he and Maggie had received—he'd followed the man back beyond the H.R. range, deciding it had been simply a warning shot. Still he was wary. But at the moment he was not planning to force any confrontation with the Rhodes men or the Stringers unless pushed to it.

It was halfway through the forenoon now as he walked Duke past the bank, the butcher shop, Mrs. Mary Shawn's Notions Store for Women, on down to Arhammer's Livery where he dismounted, stripped

Duke and gave him a good rubdown, though he wasn't all that much in need. Still, it gave him a chance to be around his friend, while he talked to him and told him a couple of things that were going on. He had always found this 'conversation' helpful when he was trying to figure something out. Duke was a great listener, and as he told one liveryman who had come upon him one time, Duke didn't interrupt.

"That be why he'd smart enough to be a hoss and not a person," the oldster had told him drily.

At Arhammer's Livery he found another oldtimer, likely a former wrangler or hand of some sort who'd known better days and was 'taking the sunshine and working out his time' right now. He took a liking to Duke right off, and Clint was glad to see that he was leaving the big black horse in able hands.

When he was done with the brisk rubdown and had spilled oats and forked hay, he checked his saddle and rigging, and finally satisfied—having used these simple activities as a means of working out his thoughts—he took off for Main Street, to see what he could turn up. He had a pretty good notion that tomorrow, when he rode onto HR range, he would find what he was looking for. He also knew that Ham Rhodes and his men were well onto that, and would be ready for him.

He had just gone a few yards away from the livery when a gnarled voice called him from the tall, wide doorway.

"You headin' uptown, mister?"

It was Link Arhammer, the grizzled, busted-up range rider and bronc stomper, now hostler for the town who was standing there framed in the entrance to his livery.

The Gunsmith stopped, turned, and regarded the gaunt old man standing under his chewed up stetson hat with a big chunk of brim missing.

"That is so," he said.

The hostler threw an eye up ahead toward the town and came closer, moving slowly for he had a game leg and an old, badly set fracture of his hip both of which had resulted in a limp, a kind of wobbling even when he was standing still, and all accompanied by much random swearing about anything at all. And to which nobody ever listened. Franklin "Link" Arhammer's rusty humor was accepted as part of him, like his clothes, his bad teeth and breath, and his acid comments on whatever it occurred to him to comment on.

"You watch yer back then," he said, as he half-staggered toward where Clint had stopped. "I heerd things, like you do when you're minding yer own bizness but something keeps nagging at you, and you can't help hearing stuff around, like in my line of work. You know what I mean?"

Clint nodded. "I do."

"Then you watch yer backtrail. Fact, it ain't my business, but you look like a decent young feller, and I'd say why don't you ride on out of town 'fore you get into something like real trouble."

By now Clint realized the man had been put up to it.

"You can tell whoever it was told you to pass that on to me to come see me personally and tell me just that. If he'd like to take that notion to do that. But for now, tell him whoever he is, that I am staying here. I am the new ramrod for the Bar Z spread, the Denzel outfit. You got that, have you?"

The hostler looked at Clint really grim then. He nodded. Clint knew he was just doing what he'd been told. Nevertheless, he held his ground, looking hard at the old man.

"Good enough then." The hostler started to turn, but then turned back. "I have gived you the message." He took a couple or three steps forward. "Here's another." And his voice was considerably lower. "If you happen to to go into the No Return, watch it. I mean— watch it!"

Clint nodded. " 'Preciate it, mister."

"Name's Link, young feller. Link Arhammer. I have heard about you. Hank Denzel was a good man." And he turned abruptly then, almost losing his balance and ambled back to his livery.

SIX

In "Lively Jim" Danny's No Return Drinking Establishment and Gaming Hall the boys were "living it up," as the local newspaper *The Whisper* had so often described such "doings" in that unique environment. The betting was strong and the crowd was growing since Heavy Harry, the chief dispenser of refreshment on the sober side of the long mahogany bar, had made the announcement that bets would be taken on the old sourdough being able to get his glass of whiskey to his mouth without spilling it.

It was Snake River Bill under all that hair, leather, dirt, sweat, chewing tobacco. An astonishing figure, already fabled for his mere presence, not to mention the numerous sulphuric utterances that dropped with frequency and good aim into the surrounding environment. As "Lively Jim" Danny had now and again observed, "A man don't know where to start looking for that feller in all that there."

Another observer of Wingtree social life offered the observation that if Snake River ever made the mistake of taking a bath he'd freeze to death stepping out of the water from the unaccustomed contact with fresh air. Others minded the time Bill had taken a load of 20-gauge in his chest and withers while drinking even more heavily than usual, and that since that moment he'd been afraid to sober up for fear he'd drop dead of lead poisoning.

The moment Clint walked into the No Return he spotted the short, stubby man who was presently the center of attention. He was bent over his glass of whiskey, supported by his forearms on the bar. Heavy Harold had filled the short glass to the brim.

Clint worked his way closer and ordered a beer, then stood back a bit so that he could quietly observe what was going on.

"Ten dollars says he can't," somebody said near him.

"I bet he can," another voice said. "I bet he can lift that there whiskey 'thout losin' a single drop! You got twenty'll fade that?"

"I bet he can't even lift the fuckin' glass, never mind spill it," another man said, but this observation was lost in the general hullabaloo.

"C'mon, Bill! What you gonna do? Set there long enough, you gonna fall in, you old bugger!"

"By God, he'll grow hair on it!"

A chuckle ran through the onlookers at the well-worn remark.

Clint had worked himself into a better place which gave him an unobstructed view of the proceedings, and he could see that Snake River Bill wasn't moving at all. It was impossible to tell whether or not he heard the comments that buzzed around him. He just continued to stand there, leaning on the bar, his gnarled forefingers and thumbs not quite touching his drink. He could have been asleep, somebody observed, except for the fact that his eyes were open.

"Could be dead," a voice said, and there was a muttering at this sage perception. "Bar's holdin' him up from dropping."

Clint saw a slight movement in the oldtimer's neck and then in his hand, and realized he was trying to move but couldn't. He said so to the man standing beside him who then leaned back on his heels and announced that it wasn't any longer a question whether Snake River could lift his whiskey glass without spilling a drop, but whether he could lift it at all. This time the remark was heard, and a delighted roar greeted this view of the situation. And Clint Adams saw that it was indeed so. Old Bill looked to be paralyzed, as someone now put it.

Suddenly a big voice said, "By God, I'll take bets on I fire this here right back of him he'll sure move!"

Clint recognized the voice, and turning saw that it was one of the Stringer twins he had encountered at the Bar Z. He was holding a six-gun in his hand and a not small circle had opened around him and Snake River Bill.

"Leave him be," Heavy Harry said from behind the bar. "Poor old bugger, he's about done for."

The Stringer twin said nothing to this, but raising his gun just slightly, and without quite pointing it directly at Clint Adams he said, "My Paw wants to see you."

"What about?" Clint said in a very quiet voice, as the room suddenly turned to stone.

"He'll tell you when he sees you."

Now the gun was pointing directly at the Gunsmith's feet, and the room's silence was emphasized by the loud ticking of the clock on the wall just above the swinging doors.

Clint said, "You tell me what he wants and then I might study on it, if I've a mind to."

Those words, spoken quite evenly and without any emotion in them whatsoever, echoed into the relentless silence of the No Return.

Clint had never felt more calm, more cool or collected in his life. He knew that the twin didn't have it in him to pull the trigger, Even though the man's big thumb now pulled back the gun's hammer.

The Gunsmith was looking right into Stringer's face, which had gone from a beefy red to a gray-white. He saw the tight lips, the eyes hard and aimed like bullets.

"Paw don't take kindly to bein' talked back to."

Heavy Harry slapped the top of the bar with his hand and said, "C'mon, Harvey. This here ain't the place for that kind of play." And he nodded toward the totally immobile Snake River Bill. "We got a bit big betting goin' on. You pick it. Is Bill there gonna lift that glass or ain't he. I be timing him now." And he took a fancy-looking horologe out of his vest pocket and dropped his eyes, trying to move everything away from the gun that was partly pointing at Clint Adams, trying to mobilize the saloon back into social activity.

Somebody sneezed. And the batwing doors swept open as a tall man with a long neck, narrow shoulders and a big drooping mustache—longhorn style—strode in. Clint took in three things at that moment: Harvey Stringer's gun dropped away, though he didn't return it to its holster, while through the mirror he saw the tall man moving towards them, and he was wearing a tin star on his shirt; and finally he checked to see once again that Snake River Bill had not moved.

"What the hell's going on here!" The voice had the tone that required an answer and right now.

"We be playing patty-cake, Marshal," Harvey Stringer said, with a cute smile on his face.

"Stringer, cut that shit—I ast you what's going on."

"I was askin' the Gunsmith here to come see my Dad, who is invitin' him out to the outfit."

"Why don't you try asking him without that particular calling card then?"

Harvey instantly returned his six-gun to its holster. He was all apology as he said, "Sorry, Marshal. I forgot."

"You also forgot I'm the sheriff, not the marshal," Harvey Stringer nodded.

The thin man had now turned to Clint, a smile on his face. "So you're the famous Gunsmith, are you." He held out his hand. "Name here is Random Gilhooley. Sorry you were inconvenienced by this hooligan here, but as you can see we got law an' order here in Wingtree. And nothin' started, nothing had to finish or whatever that old sayin' is."

But the Gunsmith had not taken Gilhooley's hand. Instead, he had pretended not to notice it as he turned back to the bar and picked up his glass of beer.

"Good enough, Sheriff. And for the record, my name is not Gunsmith, it is Clint Adams."

"Good enough then, Adams. Can I buy you one?"

"Just leaving, Sheriff. You know, I travel a good bit about the country, and I generally make it a habit to stop in with the law whenever I hit a new place—

that's got law, that is—just to let them know I'm in town. I looked for your office when I got to Wingtree, but didn't see it anywhere, and when I inquired about I was told there wasn't a sheriff, but a marshal and he was out of town. How do you figure that?"

Even before he had finished, the man with the longhorn mustache was chuckling. "Sorry, Adams. Sorry about that. Y'see, I tend to be a feller who gets a little previous now and again. And see, I'm running for sheriff; the town council is telling me they want a sheriff, not a government appointed marshal, see. And the election, well it's coming in a couple weeks. But it looks to everybody like I am gonna win it hands down. And I suspect I was just getting a little previous—like I said it's my nature to be, to do so. And I do apologize. I truly do. And I apologize to you too, Harvey Stringer. Just makin' a damn fool of myself. I am sorry folks." His voice lifted as his eyes swept to the big man behind the bar. "And to you too, Harry. Now, men, get back to yer drinkin' an' funnin'." His eyes darted toward Snake River Bill. He sniffed, raised his eyes toward the ceiling, or possibly beyond, and then walked toward the back door of the saloon. "Got to take a leak, gents."

"Well, has he moved?" A voice asked at Clint's elbow.

"About as quick as the Big Horns, I'd say," said a somber looking man with a big red nose. "Hell, he just can't make it."

Suddenly a shout went up. And all eyes turned toward Snake River Bill who appeared to be trembling as though from a severe chill.

"What's matter, Bill" Heavy Harry asked. "Here, take a snort." And he pointed to Snake's untouched glass of whiskey.

But Bill continued to tremble, and now he was actually shaking.

"Got the ague," someone said with finality.

"Or the booze has finally caught up with the poor old bastard."

A sort of sound broke from the shaking old man and all at once the room came to a standstill, drenched in astonishment.

"The old bastard's laughin' fer Chrissakes!"

"Jesus, ain't that somethin'!"

"Laughin' his goddam head off!"

Indeed Snake River Bill—and nobody really knew his last name—was now squeaking with mirth, coughing it out, his eyes filling with tears. Suddenly he bent over, his hands gripping the edge of the bar, his head down toward his feet while he shook, and finally brought his head up, crying with mirth, red-faced, sweating, and weakly pounding his fist on the bar. Everybody in the saloon stood stock still gaping at this extraordinary spectacle of human behavior.

"Sonofabitch's gone plumb loco," someone said.

"Craziern' a drunk bedbug on Sunday morning sayin' his prayers!"

"Fuck you!" suddenly shouted Bill. "Fuck all you sonsofbitches! I got mine, by God, and you kin all of yez go take a flyin', jumpin' fuck. Royal, by God!" he added. "Royal!" And wrapping his bony old hand around his glass of whiskey he raised it easy as a whistle, and with one gulp downed every drop.

Again the barroom had turned to stone. Not even breathing could be heard. There was a big grin on Heavy Harry's face as he observed Snake River Bill and those who had thought they could highjinks him. He looked over at Clint Adams who was also smiling, and one eyelid dropped in a wink.

"Snookered the bunch of yez!" said Snake River. "Thought I couldn't hold that glass steady. Hah! Eh, Heavy? Eh!" Another heaving laugh almost brought him to his knees, but he grabbed the edge of the bar in support, while he shook in silent hysteria at the crowd standing open-mouthed before him. "Dumb. Plain dumb and don't know it, by damn, even right now!" And he shook helpless against the bar, while with a flick of a finger he signaled Heavy Harry for another pouring.

"By God, the old buzzard set us up," someone said in the crowd.

"Now there be one smart feller," Snake River said with a big grin, while working his lower jaw as he chewed on an especially tasty morsel of Spark Plug. "Heh . . . heh!"

At this point Heavy Harry reached down and when he brought his hand up he was holding a bungstarter. "You gents can collect or pay on howeversome you bet. But get it done with now. The establishment here don't want—it don't *expect*—any trouble!"

The financial situation was attended to with good will and a minimum of comment or difficulty. No one had even thought of the outrageous possibility of the old codger being in on the bet. A number of accusing looks were levelled at Heavy Harry as being an accomplice, but no one voiced anything. The bungstarter in the hands of a man of Heavy Harry's muscle was not something to mess with.

At that point Clint felt more than actually saw Harvey Stringer move away from the bar. His eyes

followed him in the mirror as he pushed through the
swinging doors and out into the street.

Good riddance, Clint was thinking. And yet, something was nagging at him. Stringer had backed down
too easily. He had felt it at the moment, and he
felt it more now as his eyes began to watch Sheriff
Random Gilhooley in the mirror. Clint downed his
beer then, having decided he'd seen enough of the
No Return, yet was still aware of something incom-
plete, something that had not been settled. Yes, but
what?

His silent query was answered in the very next
moment. Looking again in the big mirror that took
up the entire wall in back of Heavy Harry, he saw
the swinging doors push open with a crack and an
old man walk in, accompanied by Harvey Stringer,
who had just left, and his twin.

The three stood for a moment letting their eyes
rove along the heads of the gathering, taking obvious
note of the Gunsmith, but not stopping there; their
eyes casually moved through the entire assemblage,
as though looking for someone.

The room had grown quiet again. Eyes were averted
from the newcomers. But their arrival was definitely
felt, Clint noted. He had expected them to confront
him, but the old man had started across the room, at
a diagonal, as though heading toward the end of the
bar away from Clint. Clint caught the swift look that
one of the twins threw in the direction of Gilhooley
who had returned, and the accompanying slight nod.
There was no question about it being a setup. Harvey
leaving the way he did, apparently was a tactic to
lower any guard that might be present, such as his
own. And then his immediate return with his twin and

the old man had to serve as a surprise. It was clear to
the Gunsmith that old Hannibal Stringer favored the
theatrical.

He saw that Gilhooley had moved to his other side,
so that he was between the sheriff and one twin. The
other twin, of course, and Hannibal, would be placed
strategically to be ready as needed.

Well, he was ready. There was nothing more to be
done. He'd been ready ever since he'd first walked
into the No Return. Now it was Harvey Stringer who
walked up to him.

"Paw wants to see you, Adams."

"That is what I know." Clint stood with his hands
at his sides, looking quietly at the twin but at the
same time taking in a lot of area on either side and
behind him.

"Let's go then," Harvey said. "No sense jawin'."

"That's right, there isn't," Clint said as he started
to move.

"Isn't what?" Harvey asked, unprepared for the man
walking right at him.

"No sense in jawin' it. So tell your old man I'll be
having my vittles at the Elk House. He can drop over
in maybe a half hour, say."

And with a nod that was barely noticeable he
stepped around the astounded Harvey Stringer and
walked without hurrying through the swinging doors.

The sunlight was hot on the back of his neck and
the backs of his hands as he walked down to the Elk
House.

The dining room at the Elk House was nearly empty.
Only a middle-aged couple eating at one of the window tables, at the far end of the large room; and also,

next to a window, a lone, rather stout man perused a newspaper while he had his coffee. As Clint sat down alongside the long wall he saw the man look at him, and noted that he was not directly in front of the window, but alongside it. Presumably, the gentleman didn't want the sun in his eyes while he was reading. His glance over at Clint revealed no apparent interest, and he had resumed his reading, twiddling the fingers of one hand. The middle-aged couple were contained in a heated discussion and evidently hadn't noticed him enter.

After giving his order to the waitress, Clint sat quietly reflecting on the events in the No Return. They had had elements of a comedy play, but at the same time he felt the note of something much more serious running like a thread through the scene. Something more had been set up than Snake River Bill's gambit. He knew that had nothing to do with the Stringers' play. But the two together had given everything a sense of unreality. And then there was the sudden appearance of the sheriff, Random Gilhooley, and his very casual behavior.

The waitress had brought his coffee and told him his steak and eggs would be right along. He was just lifting his cup when he saw the woman walk in. For an instant the sunlight, slanting through a window caught her blond hair, the regality of her walk, and at the same time something he couldn't define, but if he had to describe it, he would have called it an earthy quality, an animalism that she obviously made no effort to hide. And not so by-the-way, he was thinking, the lady was beautiful. Gorgeous! He felt his excitement growing as she glanced over at him while seating herself. And he knew there was a recognition that passed between them, though he had never seen her before.

It was a moment, hardly a second, but it had the touch of something understood, as though they had known each other already. Well, he reflected as he drank his coffee, that sort of thing did save a lot of time.

He kept his eyes more or less averted now, for he didn't want to be obvious in his interest, and finally when his steak and eggs arrived, he began to ponder on the situation with the Bar Z and the hassle with the rustlers, realizing that the Stringers had not really been planning a shootout in the crowded saloon, but were simply trying to haze him off.

Only a few moments more had passed when suddenly he saw that the waitress was approaching him, having just been attending to the other table where the pudgy man and the young blonde with the gorgeous way of moving, the soft yet definite gestures, and—though he couldn't make out the actual words—a voice that obviously matched everything else, had been deep in conversation.

"Mister Soames is asking if you would join him for a cup of coffee?"

Looking over at the other table, Clint saw the round man smiling at him. There was something gleeful in the smile that he didn't quite like. The girl, on the other hand, had her back to him. To be sure, there was no question about his refusing. He could still feel that instant of something recognized when she had glanced his way as she sat down.

Soames was standing as he arrived at the table, and Clint found it difficult to keep his eyes away from the girl as the man held out his hand and said,

"I am glad to meet you at last, Mister Adams. I'm Elijah Soames, and I'd like to introduce my business associate, I guess is the correct word—Miss Candy Thoreau."

Clint's attention quickly left the rather redfaced man with the soft brown hair plastered onto his dome-shaped head, the piercing eyes and pursed mouth which announced that he had finished speaking, and now turned to the young woman who was regarding him as though he were some article in a store that she wasn't sure of buying right now. He wanted to break out laughing. And then he realized he had heard of Candy Thoreau.

"I am happy to meet you, Miss Thoreau," he said, with a neutral smile on his face.

"Please sit down."

The waitress now brought coffee for him, and Elijah Soames offered him a cigar. The aroma reached him instantly and he knew it was first class.

"For later, of course," Candy Thoreau said with a pleasant smile.

"Thank you for reminding me, ma'am." Clint's voice was unabashedly enthusiastic as he added, "May I ask if you are somebody's mother?"

At this all three broke into laughter, and there was an immediate relaxing of the situation.

"My dear, you asked for it." Soames was grinning at her, and now started to chuckle as he reached for his cup of coffee. "You have picked a tartar here," he went on. "You see, Adams, it was Miss Thoreau— I mean to say, Candy's—notion to invite you over. But I heartily concurred." He suddenly looked around for the waitress. "But you know, I—we—interrupted your meal."

"They'll bring it over," Clint said easily. "But maybe you can tell me the purpose of your invitation? Not that I'm anything but happy to be here," he added, with a smile at the lovely creature seated within breathing distance of him. Being of course quick at observation, as well as accurate, he had instantly taken in a more detailed inventory of her physical attributes, with the easiest of glances, and with innocence. He knew that Soames was watching him.

Soames now leaned a thick elbow on the table, touched the side of his nose with his forefinger and let a moment of silence fall as he considered a reply.

"Mister Adams," he said finally. "I . . . uh . . . have a number of contacts here in Wingtree, though I am not a resident here. I have business . . ." He paused, looking into the middle distance, while Clint covertly watched the girl, interested in the expression of amusement on her face.

Soames was speaking again. "I heard of the interesting episode in the No Return—the adventure with the man known as Snake River Bill and the event that followed; namely, your confrontation with the Stringer family." A smile touched the deep corners of his mouth. "All very entertaining—I mean the part about that old trapper or whatever he is—but the concern I have is that the Stringers and their kind—well, I understand there was very nearly a shootout." He stopped abruptly, having apparently summed it up and lifted his chin, keeping his eyes on Clint.

"But not really," Clint said. "It was all pretty much staged."

"Staged?"

They were both looking at him intently.

"Sure. Put on. A show. No one in his right mind would risk a shootout in a crowded place like the No Return." He watched the surprise leaping into their faces.

"But what on earth for?" the girl asked. "I find that so hard to believe. That they would just pretend something."

"Well, it was a little more than just that," Clint said. "See, they wanted to find out how much I could take. How far they could push me. And then, of course, if anything went wrong, and someone did get hurt, they'd have me as the goat."

"But—but how did you ever come to that notion?" the girl asked, her voice, her eyes filled with amazement.

"Just by the way they were," Clint said simply.

"I must say, Adams, you are very observant. Very observant indeed." Soames leaned back and glanced at the girl, then back at the Gunsmith.

A long pause followed. Clint could feel the girl's eyes on him, but he didn't look at her. It was clear that whatever Soames had in mind Candy Thoreau knew about it. At the same time, he was trying to remember where he had heard that name. It was also interesting to discover that Soames knew so quickly about the Stringers and the action at the No Return.

"Well . . ." Soames had evidently decided on his approach.

"So, we're getting to the point," Clint said, with a thin smile.

"Sorry about that. I had to be sure." Soames was looking steadily at him.

Clint was grinning, but not with much humor. "At last," he added. "What is it you want, Soames," he said then. And turning to look at Candy Thoreau he said, "And you . . . uh . . . Candy." He said the name as though feeling it for sincerity.

She looked at him with a fresh appraisal in her eyes then. "Mister Adams, are you suggesting that you believe you may have met me someplace before?"

"I like your directness, Miss Thoreau, but I don't really know if we have ever met before today. So perhaps it's as well to leave it right here." He looked over at Soames who was leaning an elbow on the table and had his fist up against his cheek, with his face wrinkled as though he was being supported in that position.

"What you're saying, Adams, is let's get to the point."

Clint nodded.

"I want you to run for sheriff of Wingtree," Soames said. "Wingtree proper, but also a good piece of surrounding territory. The job could grow; it could grow a lot. And the rewards would be—well, substantial." He lifted his head away from his supporting fist and flicked his fingers, then dropped his hands onto the table and locked his fingers together. Clint had a close look at the big diamond ring the man was wearing on his left hand.

"I thought Wingtree already had a sheriff," Clint said.

"Obviously you are referring to Gilhooley."

"I am. He said he wasn't actually sheriff since the election hadn't been held yet, but that he fully expected to win."

"He will, unless you run against him."

"Sorry."

"Would you say why not?" Candy Thoreau asked.

"It ain't my line of work, ma'am." He pushed back his chair and stood. "Thanks for the coffee." He nodded to Soames, then glanced at the girl. "And the pleasant company." His tone was absolutely neutral.

She regarded him impassively.

"Is that your final word, Adams?" Soames asked, drawing his head back and squinting one eye as though inspecting the value of what Clint had said. "I can't understand why you turn me down."

"It is. So long." He started to leave, but then stopped.

Soames said, "I am disappointed to have you disappoint me, Adams." He cleared his throat. "You would have a free hand."

"Up to a point is what you're meaning."

Soames's smile was very thin. "I have no intention of accepting your refusal, Adams."

Clint stood there beside the table, very still. "Now you know why I am turning you down, Soames," he said. And he turned and walked out of the restaurant.

SEVEN

He knew he hadn't heard the all of it as he spent the rest of his morning getting a haircut and shave, talking to the barber, then pulling a shoe on Duke and fitting and nailing on a new one. Then he had lunch at the New Cafe, talked with the waitress, but picked up nothing in the gossip that he found useful. A visit to a couple of saloons other than the No Return also proved disappointing. Finally, about the middle of the afternoon he headed back to the room he'd engaged at the Elk House.

He had decided early to stay in town that day and night, and maybe the following day ride out to the Bar Z and check stock with Johnnie and perhaps Maggie too.

All during the time since his encounter with Soames and Candy Thoreau, he'd been checking the town for anything he could pick up on the Stringers or anyone else, and of course including Elijah Soames. But there was a damn little. People either knew almost nothing, or else were afraid of what they did know. At any rate, he now decided he'd best head back to the Bar Z and make sure that Maggie and Johnnie were all right.

Fate, or something anyway, had decreed otherwise, at least for the moment. And he felt the presentiment of this when he caught the sly look on the room clerk's face as he went past the desk. He walked slowly up the stairs, figuring it out, and then it hit him just as he reached the landing. By the time he got down to his room his felt something pounding inside him.

Just then, his natural good sense asserted itself and he checked his six-gun, and put his hand carefully on the doorknob, keeping his body well out of any line of fire.

He had already checked the quality of the knob and knew that it wasn't going to turn quietly, and he also knew he had to give it a hard and fast turn all the way before it would open. And for a flash he considered going back downstairs to brace the clerk, but decided no, he'd deal with that sneaky bugger later. Somebody had gotten to him, but the man was going to be damn sorry he hadn't given him a warning. Although, he realized in the next flash that the man had indeed given him a warning with the sneaky expression in his eyes. Of course, it was a question of how intentional that had been.

He took a breath and let it all the way out. Then, relaxed and at the same time on the razor edge of his attention all the way through his body, he slipped the key in the lock, turned it, and waited. He heard nothing; then he turned the knob and pushed the door open, quickly stepping away from the frame.

"Come in, Mister Adams."

She was sitting on the bed, leaning against the brass headpiece, with her legs stretched out in front of her.

"I apologize if I have surprised you in this way." Her smile was wholly delightful. "But I thought it would save a lot of time if we just didn't bother with all those tiring formalities. Do you agree?"

The Gunsmith didn't waste any time in even answering. He had locked the door behind him and was unbuttoning his pants as he walked towards her.

He had foreseen the shape and quality of her teats perfectly. They were firm, with rosy, erect nipples, just the right oversize for his hand, just a little more than he could encompass with his palm. Her buttocks were smooth, creamy and eager. He felt the heat under his hands as he drew her wholly naked body to him and she straddled his erect and proud organ.

"My God, you've got a pick handle there," she gasped as she rubbed her wet vagina on it. And she bit his ear. "I've got to have it! My God, I've got to have it!"

"You're getting it, my dear," he said as he laid her down on the bed and mounted.

Her legs wrapped snugly around him as he slid his great organ high and deep into her soaking, pulsating cunt. She was whimpering in his ear with utter joy as he stroked high and low, teasing it out all the way to her soaking lips, then driving in high and with his dick head rubbing up against her limit as she squirmed and bucked and fucked every exquisite stroke with him. Until he knew he would go insane if they didn't come.

And it was the kind of insanity they both wanted. He was sucking one teat now and squeezing the other with his hand, while her buttocks thrashed against the bed, which squeaked and groaned their delicious fun.

And then at last they came, squirting each other with a full hosing of what their bodies had each built up,

Clint hardly breathing as he whispered in her ear, "Candy, you're good."

"You are terrific," she gasped. "Come. For Christ sake, come! or I'm going to! But come with me, with me, with . . . me . . . with, with . . . m-m-me . . ."

And they lay there, supine and soaked in come and joy while the late afternoon sun came across the window sill and up onto the bed, which had more than earned its price, the Gunsmith reflected. Though a couple of times he'd thought it was going to smash under the exercise it had been asked to join in on.

After a moment, while they came slowly back to the room and their surroundings, she said, "My God, I knew it was going to be good, but not that good!" And she let her breath out with a long, joyful sigh. "What about you, Mister Adams?"

"I knew it was going to be that good," he said.

She blew her breath into his ear. "Smart aleck! Let's see if you can do it again then."

"Good enough. Get up on your hands and knees and I'll show you."

"Doggie-like?"

"I never thought the dogs should keep that kind of fun to themselves," he said as he entered her from behind. Sliding his rigidity all the way in side her he reached under her and took a breast in each hand and began squeezing and pumping as he stroked his cock all the way in and back, right to the lips, but at the last inch driving it forward, high and all the way to hit bottom where he held it and wiggled it back and forth while she squirmed and squealed with uncontrolled passion as she still kept time with each stroke, each

quiver, each spurt of come now as it drenched her from
his pushing, probing, throbbing cock. Until finally the
two of them all but passed out in their ecstasy, shaking,
wiggling for the last drop—and then they lay there; she
on her belly, he on top. After a time had passed, he
rolled off her, and they turned toward each other and
put their arms around their satiated bodies. And slept.

"Candy . . ."

"Clint . . ."

He sat up and looked down at her. Her head was
almost covered with the pillow, but now she moved
so that she could see him. Her blond hair was down,
falling onto her breasts and as his eyes moved down
her body she pushed back the sheet that had partially
covered her nakedness.

"I hope it still looks good," she said, and he caught
the mocking tone in her voice.

"It looks dandy, Candy."

"That there rifle you got 'tween yore legs there,
looks mighty good too, mister." Her sourdough accent
brought them both to a good laugh.

"So what else can I do for you, ma'am?" he asked,
raising up on an elbow and looking down at her.

"You can fuck me again," she said, her voice almost
a whisper, as she blinked her eyes rapidly at him, and
looked coy.

"I am figuring to do that, ma'am. But I was
wondering what it was you wanted from me. Or
perhaps it'd be better put to say what your friends
wants from me."

She sat up then, pulling the sheet around her. "You
bastard! Are you saying I came here and had sex with
you on account of Elijah!"

"Yup. That's what I know." And he looked down at her with a grin on his face. "Your pal Elijah's got good taste. Tell him I approve of his bribery. He's a smart man knowing the power of the pussy like he does."

"Bastard!"

But then immediately she reached out and touched his arm. "But a nice bastard. I've grown fond of you in our long friendship, Mister Adams."

"Tell me what your—whatever he is—wants."

"You know what he wants."

"Wants me to sheriff this town."

"Correct."

"Why?"

"You'll have to ask him."

"I told him I wasn't interested. Didn't he hear me?"

"Mister Soames doesn't hear what he doesn't want to hear."

"So—forget it."

"Why don't you do it?" she said quietly.

"I told him."

"Because you don't like the way he tried to push you around. That it?"

"That's how I said it, didn't I?"

"You're going to have to back that up to make it stick, I'm afraid."

Clint sat up on the edge of the bed. "Miss, I don't have to do anything. Now, it's been nice meeting you." He started to get dressed, suddenly filled with a presentiment of something he couldn't put into words, but he almost immediately realized what it was.

"Come lie down, honey."

He had locked the door, and shoved a chair under the knob as indeed he always did from habit. And he knew there was no way anybody could get to his window unless they were lowered from the roof.

In a moment he was fully dressed, and now he stood looking down at her.

"I think it's time for you to go home," he said. "I'm giving up this room. I ain't staying tonight."

"I'd thought we could spend the night together," she said. "You're just a fairweather rider, huh . . ."

But she made no move to get up.

And it was just in the next second that he realized what the game was. She was lying back with her head on the pillow and he remembered how she had reached down over the edge of the bed while he was dressing. It was a casual move, as though she was stretching, and he had not followed it any further. But he remembered how she had pulled the covers up over her and snuggled into her pillow while he finished dressing.

She was lying on her back now, with the covers pulled up to her chin. Her eyes were on his crotch as he stood near the bed, buttoning his pants.

"I want it again," she said.

"What kind of recommendations do you come with?" he asked, buckling his belt.

"You can check a feller named Adams."

"I'll just do that," he said, half turning away and when he turned back to face her he had his hideout in his hand.

"What the hell you doin'!" Her eyes were starting out of her head as she started to sit up, then fell back, her face flushed with shock, embarrassment, maybe fear for all the Gunsmith knew.

"All right now. Bring that gun out very, very slowly," he said. "Holding it by its barrel."

"You . . . you're crazy! Crazy like a bedbug!"

"I'm not that crazy, Candy Dandy."

"What! What are you calling me!" She was sitting up now, with the covers pulled up to cover her body.

"I want both hands out," Clint said. "I am calling you Candy Dandy. What you used to call yourself back some piece of time in Omaha. Remember? Candy Dandy's House of Paradise? How could anybody forget it."

"I never saw you before in my life! What the fuckin' hell you spewin' about, you sonofabitch!"

"Both hands out," he said. "That's it. Keep them that way."

He moved closer and suddenly reached up and grabbed the bedclothes that she was holding to cover her body as she sat there at the head of the bed, and yanked.

The gun was lying beside her.

"I never saw that thing before. How the hell did it get there!"

"It was under the bed where you hid it."

"I never! You put it there! I never!"

"What were you going to do?" he said as he put his hideout away and then broke the derringer and dropped its load onto the bed. "Were you going to shoot me? Or what?"

"I was going to take you to Soames. That's what!"

"Why?"

"Because he told me to do that. That's why!"

"No, you weren't. You were going to hold me here and then call out to whoever's out in the corridor. And they'd work me over. Right?"

She was suddenly covering her eyes with her hands, her body shaking. As she sobbed.

"Cut it out," Clint said, his voice sharp. "You don't fool anybody with that act. Why din't you just slug me while I was asleep. Or let them in then?"

"Because I could tell you weren't asleep, you bastard."

"Good thing I wasn't—huh," he said.

"Shit . . ." All at once she looked dejected.

"You can't win 'em all," the Gunsmith said. "Now get your clothes on and go out and tell those fellers out there, or wherever they are that they'd better try something else. And as for your pal Soames . . . Well, I'll send him a message. It is this. Tell him I am with the Bar Z, the Denzel outfit. I'm the foreman and I will be protecting the Bar Z interests. You can tell that to him. And make sure the sonofabitch hears you!"

He stood there watching her dress which she did quickly, her anger rising with each movement she made. When she was done she strode to the door, but it was locked.

"Are you going to let me out of here!"

"I think we'll go out together," Clint said.

"You bastard!"

He grinned at her. "Sweetheart!"

"My dear, I can think of no better man to quote than he who is known as 'The Fighting Quaker'— Mordecai Harrison Mills, who so aptly pointed out that young men without money have only one avenue open to them for making a fortune: they must connect themselves with capitalists. And of course, the best place to invest capital is in the West." Elijah's small, softly thick hands opened, revealing palms with innumerable lines. "I can offer no more sage observation than this." He grinned at her, at Candy Thoreau who was sitting on the edge of the wide bed totally—and as he observed—delightfully naked.

They had just finished one of their finest sexual bouts, and each was revelling in total satisfaction. Although neither, at the same time, for an instant had forgotten the main purpose in life. Elijah, she thought, was so good at putting it into words.

Indeed, Elijah Soames had studied his situation, and that of American capitalism in depth, height, and width. And he had secured his "philosophy" through action. What he proposed worked. Thus, he had learned while building the Indiana-Pacific railroad that more capital could be collected from organizing land companies, laying out towns, and selling lots than he could ever get from the railroad itself. Nor was it any concern to him that such towns might wither and die because they had no solid economic base.

Candy Thoreau, graduate of Annie Chambers's famous Kansas City brothel, knew her man to the last penny. She had learned much from the fabled Annie. And she had brought her own special talents—not only monetary, but sexual to help her along the way. As with Elijah. She had met him at Annie's place, where all the rich went, even such as Jesse James, not to mention a number of bankers, financial wizards, and executives. In short, Elijah Soames. She had done well for a poverty-stricken Irish child raised in the slums of New York City.

She knew she had Elijah's confidence. Not his complete trust, but ninety percent. It was plenty. One should not be greedy; moreover, she was sufficiently astute to know that once you believed you knew everything about someone else, no matter how close they were, then you were in trouble.

She was well aware of how Elijah had bypassed the pleasant little town of Moray Springs when he built his railroad fifty miles south of Omaha. The land around Moray Springs had been too expensive for handsome profit and so he'd gone further out and acquired large blocks of land for eighty cents an acre. When he built his railroad south he bypassed Moray Springs for his new town of Moray City where he made large profits by selling off lots. Only a few months later, Moray Springs lost the county seat to Soames's Moray City and as a result it died. Soames's Moray City was on a railroad and Moray Springs was not. Simple as apple pie, as Candy saw it. And as Elijah told it.

And that wasn't all, she'd discovered. The next town in line was Linksville, and Soames's first move was to send an emissary there to let the citizens understand that it was necessary that they raise $175,000 for the new railroad or the town would be bypassed. Linksville's citizens raised the money and Elijah strung his tracks alongside the town, as promised. However—and this was the part that Candy admired so much—he built the depot across the river so that he could sell lots in his new town of Linktown.

Elijah was fond of telling some of these things to her, and she delighted in hearing them. But, for a fact, she did get a bigger kick from ferreting out her material on her own. It was exciting. Of course he knew about it. His "Enterprise", as he called his business, connected everything that happened back to the man with the big money fist: to Elijah Soames.

At the moment, as they lay quietly in bed, Elijah was pondering on his moves in relation to Wingtree.

His aim was to build the place up and sell it to the Denver & Rio Grande, knowing full well that he could make a better deal running rails further south. He had at first thought that Wingtree was the area he wanted for his new enterprise, building south and west, but he had realized that running his line south of Wingtree could be done faster, in other words before the Denver & Rio Grande got wise to the fact that there was very likely gold in the southern area. At any rate, even if there wasn't gold, he'd make a profit, for the track laying would go quicker south of Wingtree. At the same time, it gave him much satisfaction to give the Denver & Rio Grande a kick—you know where—thus evening it for their having turned down his proposition to run a line for them a good three years ago. Elijah did not take sweetly to having his proposals rejected. Especially by idiots.

"So I take it you haven't any news on the chance of gold," she was saying now as she stretched her full length on the bed, while his eyes roved over her creamy skin, her large pink nipples, and her soft, luxuriant bush. He especially admired her thighs.

"No news. But there is good news afoot in Wingtree." There was a teasing laughter in his eyes as she sat up and looked at him. He was still naked, and he sat with his hairy legs hanging over the edge of the bed.

"What? Can you tell me?" And she reached behind him to feel just where the crack between his buttocks began.

"There might be a cattle war."

"Cattle war? Why is that good news? I don't understand."

"I know you don't, my dear. But it's elementary. Ham Rhodes is the big cattle chieftain around this part of the country." He paused briefly. "And old Old-man Hannibal Stringer, with his four lusty boys, is the outlaw chieftain, dealing in stolen cattle, stolen horses—with a sideline of railroad holdups, and possibly a bank here and there." He opened his hands. "It can be only a matter of time before— well, need I say more."

"Is this why you wanted Clint Adams to run for sheriff?"

"I don't especially want him to run for sheriff, it's rather that I want him to work for me."

"Dearie, I don't think he's the type."

His face clouded instantly as he stared at her, searching for disloyalty. But there was none. She looked as innocent as her name. Candy.

"Don't be angry, Lije. I was only trying to see the situation more clearly. There must be a way to work things out the way you feel they should be worked out."

He nodded, a slight smile touching his thin lips, satisfied that there was no disloyalty about. "The Enterprise needs him in a certain way; that is to say I need to make sure that he will mind his own business, that he will be inactive. But I fear that he is mixed up in the rustling situation, since someone he knew was unavoidably shot and killed not very long ago."

"Aah! I see." She sniffed. "So that's where he comes in. He could upset the wagon."

"He certainly could. If he takes it into his head to tangle with either the Stringers or Rhodes, he could mess up the whole Enterprise plan. That—in a nutshell, my dear, is why I suggested your involvement with the gent."

There was a pause, while he studied her. He was thinking of getting up for a cigar.

"I feel very much that you're asking me something," she said as he got to his feet.

He didn't answer until he'd taken the cigar out of his coat pocket and returned to the bed. "I am, my dear. Something very important."

"You want me to try again."

He didn't answer for he was busy lighting his cigar. Then, looking at her as he released his first small cloud of smoke, and watched it rising toward the ceiling, he said, "My dear, you can read minds."

She had risen and had walked to the bureau where there was a mirror. She stood there looking at her figure from the front, then from the side.

"Do you think I'm attractive, Lije?" And she turned back to face him, a teasing smile on her lips.

"That is a foolish question, my dear. It should not be addressed to me in the first place, but to him." He pointed down to his half erect penis, which had started to stir into action while she was looking at herself in the mirror.

"He doesn't look so interested, now that you mention it."

"I think he is," Elijah said spreading his legs a little while his erection firmed to its limit. "That tell you anything?"

"Maybe."

"Come here." He nodded toward the bed.

"I might think about that," she said moving slowly toward him, while his organ stood like a tree between them.

"I want you to suck him a long time," he said.

"Do you?"

"Yeah, I do. Do it like a lady."

"Ladies don't suck cocks."

"Then don't be a lady."

His legs were spread as he remained seated, and she was standing between them.

"Come on. Do it any way you like, like a lady or not."

"You like me to be a lady, don't you."

"I do."

"It's part of the fun, isn't it."

"If you say so. Anyhow," he went on as he leaned back. "Show me." He closed his eyes, his hands were behind him, bracing him on the bed as he spread his legs farther apart. "You are a lady, aren't you."

"I am," she said, moving in on him and kneeling on the floor.

"Good. That's what I want you to be. That's what I need you to be."

"For the Enterprise," she said. "For the Enterprise, and also for him," he said, pointing his thumb down at his erection.

He didn't hear the slight crack in her voice as she said, "I am a lady." And she took his rigid organ in her fist.

"I know that," he said.

"I want you to tell me."

There was a pause and then he said, "You're a lady."

"Then take that fucking cigar out of your mouth, Godammit!"

EIGHT

It had taken a lot of jawing, but with some help from Johnnie he'd been able to talk her out of coming along. She'd sure not given in easily, but finally his argument that she was needed at home, because it wasn't wise to leave the place unguarded, won out.

"All I can say is that none of those whoever-they-are-people had better show up here," Maggie muttered darkly.

Clint knew she was half joking, but he played it straight. "There's no reason why anyone should come by here," he said. "And anyway, we won't be gone that long." He was looking straight at her as he spoke. "Anyway, if somebody did show up, I want you to not even look at them or say a word, but get on that chestnut pony and hightail it for Rhodes's place." He paused, watching her. "I'm sure nobody's going to come by. They don't know we won't be around—Johnnie and myself. And we don't aim to be that long checking their stock. I only want to check some of it, not the whole outfit. At least for a start."

"All right. All right."

But he could see that she still wasn't satisfied.

"You really want to come along, don't you," he said.

"They're my cattle aren't they?"

"You want me to stay here?"

"No! No. Well, I don't know what I mean. I'm sorry." And her eyes dropped. "I'm sorry, Clint. I— it's, well it's just been a lot since Dad . . . was shot. Forgive me. I was just acting a bit childish, and trying to get you to take me along." Suddenly she grinned, and he saw the tears drying in her eyes. "I . . . I was just being foolish."

He was smiling at her. "You know, I tell you what I'd like to do. How we'll handle this. I mean, if you still want me as foreman of the Bar Z."

"But of course I do. Oh, I'm sorry."

He stood looking at her. They were in the kitchen and the sunlight was breaking through the window and spilling onto their coffee mugs.

"Tell me what you want to do. Whatever you say is all right with me. I really mean that."

"I'll go alone. I'll leave Johnnie with you. The two of you can start a count of what you've got here."

"Now, Mister Adams!" She was wagging her finger at him. "I knew—I just knew you were going to ace the situation somehow." But she was laughing.

And in the next moment he was laughing with her.

"I should have figured it out easily. You just want to be shut of us. I might have known it! You want to be alone!"

"No I don't."

"Then why? . . ."

"When I'm engaged in something that might be dangerous—yes," he admitted. "But—like not now."

Then he had his arms around her.

"Is there time?" she asked suddenly soft as she nestled against him.

"We'll take time."

"What if . . ."

He cut her short. "I asked Johnnie to check the feed up around Bryce Coulee. We'll be pushing them through there when we go for the summer range."

"Mister Adams, you do think of everything."

"It's my nature," he said as he led her into her bedroom and shut the door.

"But don't you have to get on over to the HR?"

"That's right. I do! Why, I almost forgot!" And he dropped his arm which had been around her waist and turned away, as though about to leave.

"Beast!"

He had his arms around her again. And this time he didn't take them away; at any rate, not till he was ready to undress her.

"Is there time?" she whispered as she lay down on her bed with his body on top of her.

"Miss, you've already asked that question. Didn't you listen to the answer?"

"Tell me again," she whispered, hardly able to get the words out as his hands began pulling off her clothes.

"We'll take time, I said. Remember?"

But she didn't answer. He had closed her mouth with his as, still half dressed, he entered her with his pulsing erection.

• • •

This time their lovemaking seemed to surpass even what they'd adventured into before.

"Why is it that each time is better than the last?" she asked him.

"That's the way it is in Paradise," he said.

"Let me be on top this time."

"Any time you want."

She was already straddling him, rubbing her thick bush along his hard member, but not yet allowing entry, as she reached behind herself and stroked it with her fist, then all at once she slipped him in between her wet lips and sat down on it with a squeal of delight while Clint thought he would lose his mind as well as the load that had been building. But he held onto it, wanting to bring it to the final exquisite split-second before the grand release.

Now they were stroking in perfect rhythm as she rose and dropped on his big, hard stick while his hands gripped her thrusting buttocks, and their tongues sucked each other's with their mouths sealed together in joy.

She knew just how far to raise up and still keep his organ inside her, just at the tip of entry, and then working down till their pubic bones were sealed together and they squirmed and then thrust and stroked, going faster and faster, and deeper and higher, and together more madly in the exquisite panting, bucking crescendo until the explosion came, and she was flooded and he emptied himself totally. As he subsided, still inside her, there was not a single drop of come left in him.

"Well . . . ?"

The lone word came hard from beneath the wide

brim of Ham Rhodes's Stetson hat. It came past the tight lips, out of the shadow thrown down on the hard face, backed wholly by the resolute stance of the HR owner.

"No hide, no hair of him," said Ty Schwinneger as he stepped down from the frisky little buckskin pony who was sweating some; Ty had ridden him hard to deliver his "no news" report.

"Shit." The leathery face under the big hat was motionless, save for the movement transferring the wooden lucifer from one side of the harsh mouth to the other. "What's that sonofabitch up to, you reckon."

The question, however, was not asked of the foreman who was looking totally puzzled, as he watched his employer's reaction to the news that no one had seen a sign of Clint Adams, the man known as the Gunsmith.

"Reckon he must of changed his mind," Ty finally said, with his eyes careful on his boss. No telling how the man would be taking it. For it looked by golly like that Gunsmith feller was trying to pull a sandy. Like saying he was riding out to inspect brands and saying it hard too, and then not showing up. By God, just not even showing up.

" 'Less somethin' could of happened to him," Ty said, suddenly finding an opening for a little light.

"Uh—uh." This utterance, which was more sound than actual verbal discourse, settled the question with a finality that only a man such as Ham Rhodes could bring. And there was more.

"Sonofabitch is up to somethin', I'll be bound." The boss of the HR said those words as though testing them for their ability to express what he was thinking and feeling.

"The hell . . ." The ramrod of the HR scuffed dirt with the toe of his boot. And spat thoughtfully, turning his head slightly away from his employer, yet not aiming at anything.

Silence. Silence within the ticking silence of the moment that Ham Rhodes had prepared for the confrontation with the man known as the Gunsmith but who now had simply not shown up. The fox! The goddam snake!

And so the two of them—the rancher and his ramrod—stood there in the silence that held, but did not communicate their thoughts. Each knowing though that they were up against someone who wasn't afraid. A man not only not afraid of his fellow man, but a man not afraid to make a mistake. The kind of man Ham Rhodes favored, in fact. And he was telling himself just that as he stood pondering in the hot sun, while his foreman waited.

"You better get on out to see how the men are," Rhodes finally said. "Maybe he'll show up, maybe he won't. But we'll go ahead with our plan, and the way I told you."

Ty Schwinneger was standing absolutely still save for his boney jaws which were chewing fast as a prairie dog's.

"I'll tell the boys to start the gather then." He paused, squinting at his boss. "Soon—huh?"

"Not soon. Right now."

The foreman's jaw dropped. "You mean . . ."

"I mean right now. Start moving everything that's got four legs to the back range. Then well before sunup we'll start moving them."

"To the mountain?"

Ham Rhodes had leaned his cane against the side of

the big horse corral, and now, for some inexplicable
reason, the stick suddenly fell to the ground.

Schwinneger automatically made a move in the
direction of the cane to pick it up. There was no
servility in his movement; he was simply helping a
man with a game leg, like he would expect the same
if the positions had been reversed.

"Leave it!" And Ham Rhodes was standing on his
two legs right smack in front of him, his thumbs
hooked into his belt, his mouth a thin, hard line.

Then—"We'll start 'em up well before dawn.
Tomorrer."

"But I figgered . . ."

"I said toward the mountain—toward it . . ." And
the boss of the HR looked hard on the man who had
been ramrod for all these years and still didn't appear
to know his ass from a salt lick.

Suddenly Schwinneger's face cleared. " 'Course,"
he said. "Sure. 'Course." And a grin appeared and
his whole body took on a new quality while his boss
watched.

"You know what to do now."

"Gotcha . . ." And all at once the foreman's knobby
jaws were chewing fast as a prairie dog's. And there
was no indecision at all in the way he checked the
buckskin's cinch, and then head stall, and mounted.
Buck caught the flavor of it and started to step nimble
and fast for a minute, snorting, like he was fixing to
maybe even buck, or anyway crowhop, until his rider
cut him a couple of good ones, and he simmered down,
though still with his ears out sideways and snorting
and rolling his big eyes.

Looking down at his boss standing there without
his cane, Ty Schwinneger touched the brim of his

stetson hat with his forefinger, still holding his reins in that hand, and kneed Buck in the direction he wanted to go.

As he rode off he was sure Ham Rhodes had given him a nod. Almost invisible, for sure. But that was the way the man was. Never moved more than was necessary. Or spoke extra. A man of few words, few movements. A man always close to himself. Ty Schwinneger liked that in a man. Hell, it was what separated the hay from the straw, as his old man used to tell him long ago, back in Minnesota, on the farm he'd run away from.

Ham Rhodes watched him leave. He was thinking how the Gunsmith feller was maybe going to be a problem bigger than he'd figured. Good enough. It might be he was just the thing needed to keep himself sharp for what had to be done. Maybe. And why not? A man needed always something to keep him on the edge. Sure the Stringers filled that place. But they weren't like this man Adams. Gunsmith. A name, that.

He reached to his pocket for a cigar and started to walk slowly toward the house. Yes, by jingo! Maybe that Gunsmith feller could be gotten use out of, after all. He was grinning inside as he reached the door of his house.

He suddenly remembered something, and turned back to take a look. His cane was still leaning against the corral poles. He turned back to the house. He was grinning more deeply as he opened the door and walked carefully in.

Elijah Soames had plans for a large office, housed in a large building that had not yet been built. In the absence of such a structure, which he would soon push through, the man who was planning the Enterprise held his meetings in the large room above Harry Hatfield's Undertaking Parlor and Carpentry Shop. A good place; it was spacious, there was adequate furniture (a large desk and chairs), and a table with a green baize top—useful for a game of cards or a roll of the dice.

Elijah favored the dice. In fact, years earlier, as a boy and young man, he had played the Mississippi riverboats. His ability to switch tops and flats, second deal, and use readers, earned him the reputation as a deadly opponent at the tables. Unfortunately, his well-earned fame eventually turned into notoriety, and Elijah found his days numbered. Anyhow, it had been time to move beyond the Mississippi. His ambitions were sighting on bigger game. And—no question about it—the opening and expanding of the West offered an El Dorado of pillaging to the resourceful, not to mention the ruthless. Elijah proved himself no amateur at seizing opportunity and riding for the top money.

At the moment the man who had created, nursed, and was about to bring to fruition, the great idea, the plan, and more than likely, the historical event—the Enterprise—was sitting back in his easy chair, behind his big desk, examining his fingernails. It seemed to the others present that all Elijah Soames' attention was on this grooming activity, such was his concentration. But now, biting at a hangnail, his eyes rose to take in the group seated before him. And they quickly realized that his attention had been with them all along.

"They" were the Wingtree Council sitting there in a semi-circle. Josiah Boles, Rick Hemming, Tom Swindown; the principal citizens of the town, the ones most concerned with Wingtree's future, and the ones that set the tone, the financial possibilities, and the course of growth and development; in short, the men in charge of the community's place, and even its history. Elijah Soames had told them how important they were. And they believed him; remembering, of course, that Mr. Soames was more important, and that they were all servants of The Enterprise, the great effort that was helping to transform the wilderness into a productive and wholly useful society.

Rick Hemming had just finished relating his latest efforts in raising money for the church which was in the process of being built. Plus, money was needed to build another room onto the schoolhouse. Josiah Boles had spoken of the expansion of his hardware business, and Tom Swindown—the suspected half-breed—mentioned his new loan-making policy, which in fact, he had secretly discussed and worked out with Soames the day before the meeting.

Elijah had finished with his hangnail, and was rubbing the offending place on his middle finger with his thumb.

"Well, we seem to be well caught up all-around, gentlemen. Good then, but we still have our central line of effort to throw our weight into."

"The railroad," Josiah Boles said softly.

"First . . ." Elijah lifted his thick forefinger. "First there is the election." And he lifted his thin eyebrows and looked at each of the three in turn; his whole appearance was one of scolding their forgetfulness.

"Ah, of course," said Boles with a sigh. "Our . . . uh, friend."

"Random," said Rick Hemming with a wry look on his cleanshaven face.

And Tom Swindown grimly added, "Gilhooley."

"The point is, gentlemen, that it looks as though Gilhooley is going to be our next sheriff."

"The damn fool!" snorted Boles.

"What about Adams," said Swindown. "I thought . . ."

"I've spoken with the Gunsmith fellow" Elijah said, speaking slowly, and with care. "And I've decided he's not really the man we want, need." His glance swept slowly over the trio. "However, he is still a factor. Adams. And this is, in fact, the main purpose of our meeting."

"I feel you're saying you don't trust the man, Elijah," Josiah Boles said. "Is that so?"

"It is." Soames cleared his throat. "I do not trust him, but that doesn't mean we can't make use of him."

"Sounds to me like a tough one," Boles said.

There was a smile playing at the corners of Elijah's mouth. "I feel that rather than it being a disappointment, that in truth, a small bonanza has fallen into our hands."

"How so?" Tom Swindown asked. His face was as dark as it always was. And his attitude matched it, dark with suspicion. "I hear that man is smart, and he is certainly tough. We've all heard things about him, like how he faced down the Stringers in the No Return. And other things too. I'm for going extremely careful with that man, thank you."

It seemed all at once everyone realized that the conversation had run out. Silence had taken over, silence and the fading sunlight coming through the filthy window glass.

The silence lengthened, and gradually it began to occur to them that Soames was acting as though waiting for something. But for what?

And it was Soames who heard it first: the presence of someone in the small passageway outside the room.

Then there came a loud knock at the door. Two knocks, the second following hard on the first.

Elijah Soames inclined his head in the direction of Rick Hemming who, with a swift clearing of his throat, called out for the person to come in.

A tall, thin, wiry man entered. He was wearing a black shirt, a black hat with a clean, well-cared-for appearance to it. In fact, he was dressed in black from the waist up, and in dark grey from the waist down, save that his heavily tooled boots were black.

"Come in, Mister Anders," Soames said. "Come in. Take that chair. And uh, let me introduce you."

There was a slight shifting of chairs to make room for the visitor who now took his place. All eyes were on him as he sat down. Tall, lean as a rope, and graceful in movement. This was how Josiah Boles summed him up. Hard, definitely no man to argue with; the kind you let alone unless you wanted big trouble, was Tom Swindown's assessment. As for Rick Hemming, the "man of God" saw the visitor in biblical terms: a man wicked all the way through, even a servant of the Devil himself. But at the same time he could be taken as one of those hard, inflexible ones whose conversion to the true way made glory in heaven. Ah, yes. It was always so, the reverend reflected. It was the tough ones that tested one's mettle in the service of the Lord. Well, he could flex his mental muscles, his emotional power, the clean, swift stroke of his own belief and devotion.

And then to everyone's astonishment, Elijah said that the meeting was over.

"Mister Anders and myself have a few things to

talk over. And I believe we're all in agreement with
what we were discussing. So—we'll have another
get-together soon." And he stood up. The others rose
to their feet, covering their surprise as best they could
with idle talk, scratchings, and reaching into and out
of pockets.

Elijah made a motion with his palm for the visitor
to remain seated, though Anders hadn't stirred.

In another moment they were all gone, and now
Elijah Soames returned to his desk and sat down and
looked at the man seated comfortably in the only
other armchair in the room, besides his own. Josiah
Boles had been sitting in it when the newcomer had
arrived, and at a signal from Soames, had surrendered
it to the tall, wiry man with the six-gun riding low on
his left hip.

The man named Anders leaned back in his armchair
now and with eyes half-lidded regarded his host who
was busy cutting the end off a cigar.

"That's a good looking smoke, I'd say." The voice
was cold, frugal; it was very clear that the speaker
expected to be heard without repeating himself.

"Like one?" Soames cocked an eye.

Anders didn't answer. He simply watched out of
his rather small green eyes as his host reached to his
pocket and took out a cigar and passed it over.

Watching Anders as he picked up the cigar and
prepared to light it, Elijah said, "Well, those are the
main citizens of town. There are others. But those
three make the mare go."

"But I am dealing with yourself," Anders said. His
voice was strong, decisive, and it was again obvious
to Soames, who had met him only once before, that
the man wouldn't hesitate to stoop—or, as the event

might call for—rise to anything at all in executing his desired plan. He had never seen such cold eyes in a human being, he decided, and there was even a slight tightening somewhere inside him as he watched Anders lighting his cigar.

"And I need to know just what it is you want," he went on, blowing out smoke and leaning back a little in his chair. Elijah caught the cold laughter in his eyes, which was lacking anywhere else in his body.

"It will be a difficult job," Soames said.

"I think I can decide how difficult it is," Anders said.

Elijah checked the retort that sprang to his lips, controlling himself by remembering his aim.

"The job will first of all require patience. A lot of patience," he added, sticking to the line he had decided for his approach, and not allowing his intention to change simply because of the other's arrogant attitude.

"Tell me." The green eyes looked small as shirt studs. The lips barely moved as the words appeared to be released, rather than spoken.

"I will probably want someone to be—uh, taken care of."

"Killed. That's what you told me last time. And that's what was done. That right? You got any complaints from last time?"

"None. But it's because of that event that now I feel a certain need for special care."

"You meet my price, and there won't be anything to worry about. Cold, hard money on the barrelhead. And afterwards it'll be an easy ride home."

Suddenly, Elijah decided on a new tack. He bent down and opened the little drawer near his right leg, and withdrew a bottle of whiskey, then bending again, he brought up two glasses.

"A touch of the creature might be a good way to seal our understanding."

Leaning forward, Anders accepted the glass of whiskey, taking it in the same hand that was holding his cigar. Elijah felt a sudden fascination for the way the man moved. Well, he knew he had the right party. He had used Anders before on a certain job, and he had never met anyone that cool.

"You understand," Anders was saying, "That you've hired me. You expect me to kill somebody, without leaving any notion you're connected. Now I've told you my price, and I've told you that if you decide suddenly not to kill this person . . . you've still got to pay me. That is understood—yeah?"

Elijah thought he detected the trace of a German accent in those words but it didn't make any difference; he let it go. What counted was to have somebody on hand to take care of Adams, should the occasion arise. The rest of the situation Stringer and his boys could handle. But it was obvious that Hannibal and his wily sons weren't in the same class as the man who was known as the Gunsmith,

Anders raised his glass. "We'll drink to the first payment, which has been received. And we agreed that then the second and final payment would come after the work is done; or not done, as you might decide against it at a certain moment."

"Right. That is correct."

"There's a change in that. See, I might have to leave pronto, and get plumb out of the country and fast. So that final payment will come just before."

"Before!"

"Before."

"But we agreed . . ."

"That I know, but that's why I am changing it now. I got to think of how I'll be getting away, and I won't have time to diddle around running after yourself, who might be hard to find if there's a lot of excitement, especially . . . Well, never mind it. I just say I need to be paid before." And he looked levelly at his host.

"I don't like it, Anders. We made an agreement."

The man in the armchair raised his glass, gave a little nod of his big head and downed the liquor.

"Adios, as they say down in Old Mexico."

"But you've already been paid like we both agreed upon. Dammit!"

"Sorry, mister . . ." And suddenly the tall, thin man was up on his feet.

Elijah managed to control himself; in fact, he was a bit surprised to discover he wasn't as angry as he thought he ought to be. But of course he couldn't allow anything to get in the way of the execution of the Enterprise. His Enterprise!

"All right. All right," he said. "But you'll have to wait till tomorrow. When the bank's open."

"What time?"

"Come at noon. At which time I'll have more specific orders for you. Including who I might want you to kill."

"I already know who it is, Soames."

"How? How could you know that?" Elijah demanded, taken aback by this bit of news.

"I learned just one thing in school, Soames: how to put two an' two together." He suddenly grinned revealing a gap where a tooth was missing. "You're getting off easy. If I'd known who it was before we agreed on the price, I'd have doubled it. And don't you forget this," he added, standing tall and hard directly in front of Elijah Soames. "That if you decide not to go ahead, you still have to pay me."

"I know. You've told me that already."

The man named Anders grinned as he walked to the door and opened it, saying, "I'll see you tomorrow."

"Make it here. And don't let anybody see you coming. Not even any of those who were here before."

His visitor nodded, and was gone.

Elijah returned to his desk and sat down with a long sigh. The door to an adjoining room opened behind him and he heard her come in. He didn't turn around, but just waited until she was standing before him.

"I want to say I think you handled that very, very well."

He felt the rush of pleasure all the way through him.

"It wasn't easy," he acknowledged. "Some people are just too damn greedy."

"It is a lot of money, no question," she said, as she picked up the bottle and poured into his glass. Setting the bottle down, she lifted his glass and making the gesture of a hearty toast, drank.

"A lot of money," she repeated.

Elijah was smiling. "If he should live to spend it, I guess it is," he said.

She caught it instantly and beamed at him. "You know something, Lije. I have always thought how you're not only a tough man to do business with— not that I personally would know—but I have eyes and ears and, well, like I said before, I do admire the way you handle things."

He had reached down to his cupboard and come

up with another glass and was now pouring himself a fresh drink.

He put down the bottle, raised his glass and said, "Know something, lady? So do I."

NINE

The moment the Gunsmith's shadow fell through the big doorway and spread onto the chewed-up wooden floor, Duke let out a low nicker of recognition and tossed his head, though he didn't stop eating. Old Link Arhammer had just dumped a short can of oats into the box in the corner of the hay trough and the big black gelding had needed no encouragement. And as Clint came closer he continued feeding, while some of the oats, soaked in his saliva, slipped out of his mouth and fell back into the feed box.

Clint nodded in the direction of his friend and spoke to Link Arhammer's back as he receded into the darkness of the rear of the livery.

"Anybody about looking for me, was there?" he asked.

Some sound that appeared more grunt than actual word came back from the old hostler. Clint took it to be no, or anyway nothing of any account, as he moved over to take a closer look at Duke.

"How you doing, big boy?" He ran his hand along

143

the sleek black coat, down the withers, and down the foreleg to check the new shoe. Lifting the leg, he examined his own handiwork. The shoe looked good, and he was pleased. He preferred doing his own shoeing, and he had a good notion that Duke felt the same about it.

"Feller from the town council was about lookin' for you." The words came mumbling out of the old hostler's dry lips. "Somethin' about the election."

"Did he want to know if I was going to run?"

"Run? Run for where? Why would you be runnin'? Hell, it's too damn hot to run anywheres."

"I'm sayin', was he wondering whether I'd be running for office."

"Sheriff's office—huh. Dunno what he meant. An' anyways, hown' hell can a office run. Now riddle me that!"

He came clomping in close, scratching himself with his hands deep in his ancient pockets, his overalls baggy in the crotch, like he was carrying a set of carpenter tools there, Clint was thinking.

"You got a cigar on ye?" the old man asked.

"Wish I did."

"Shit! Man can't count on a goddam soul these days." Grumbling, scratching, he approached closer, peering at Duke, then at Clint. He stood more or less still, though sniffing some, and now and again peering about, in the direction of corners, maybe into thoughts.

His crackled voice was softer as he almost whispered the words. "Feller was watchin' the place s'afternoon. Tall, thin."

"Anyone you know?"

"Never seen him before. Packing hardware, left

side, for a crossover draw. Like—butt forward."

Into Clint's mind came the picture of Luke Johnson, who wore cross-draw rigging, except he had a very strong notion that Luke was lead-dead. "Short, stocky feller was he?"

"Tall. Real lean, like a whip."

"Man shooting right handed. Huh."

"Like I said, crossover.

"How old?"

"I didn't get that close to ask him."

"You just see him the one time?"

"Nope." He paused to let fly a streak of tobacco spittle. This was followed by a scampering of little feet down the length of the livery accompanied by the old man's cussing. "Bastard! Shit! Fuck! Missed the bugger. Light in this here ain't worth a piss in hell!"

"You knew him before then."

"Didn't say so. You ast had I seen him only the oncet. But I recollect now I seen him up at Purdy's night before last; well, actually it was in the morning. Late, or early—as how you see it. Early in the morn. I'm standing at the bar having a morning eye-opener after playing draw poker half the night, an' I look up and here's this feller standing there lookin' at me. Exceptin' that his face don't say anything. He was looking at me like I was a wall or somethin'. Damndest thing."

"That the only time?" Clint asked, while still searching his memory for someone who met the description. Only in vain.

"That's the only. Yup."

"Huh." Clint studied it; for some reason he could not have explained, he felt there was something strange about the episode.

"Exceptin', no," the old hostler went on. "I did see this same feller again. Funny though."

"Why was it funny?"

"Well, this was a man who looked to be pretty fast. I mean he wasn't real old or anything." He was shaking his head, remembering something, or so it seemed to Clint Adams. "And when I got down to the livery there he was."

"So . . . ?"

"Well, like you can see, it don't take too long to walk down here. An' I know he could of easily got here 'fore meself. Exceptin' he had something different about him. And it took me couple minutes to figger he had on a different shirt. An' I wondered now why'n hell does a man change his shirt in the middle of the night like that? Well, it caught me funny. But then I got closer, on account of he was standing in the door an' he had to move for me to get in there. Then I see he had the same shirt on. So—well, I figgered it was still dark. Still the night." He sniffed, spat. "Well, anyways, there I wuz with him and his poker game, and then he wuz there down at the livery. I figgered maybe he wanted to hire a hoss." He moved suddenly closer to Clint. "Now get this. Here's something to figure. Huh! Like I reckon I said, I had a notion, just for a minute that he was like snoopin' around, especially when he started askin' question about your big black there."

"Oh he did, eh."

"I thought maybe he wanted to buy him. Others have mentioned your hoss. Hell, all you got to do is look at him and you'll see why. So maybe it was like that. I dunno. Well, I got to git me some coffee."

Clint nodded, figuring he was about to take off. But

the old boy remained right where he was. It was as though he was waiting for Clint to say something.

Except, Clint wasn't particularly interested in saying anything. He had been hoping to pick up something from Old Link Arhammer.

They stood there, the two of them, listening to the horses, the livery, the time of day, and sometimes their own insides.

"You know Elijah Soames?" Clint asked suddenly, deciding on the moment to throw it out at the old man, who was obviously trying to tell him something.

"Never heard of the feller," the old man said. And holding Clint Adams's eyes for a few seconds, he then turned and walked back into his barn.

The gesture, the words, and especially the way they had been spoken, told the Gunsmith all that he needed to know. He was smiling to himself as he started back up the street And he was thinking how silence, when "said" in a certain way, could tell a man such a whole lot, more than a whole wagon-load of words.

Ham Rhodes stood outside the cookshack watching his foreman and two men ride in from the north range. They'd been mending fence, and were packing a couple of shovels, wire, and some fencing tools for tightening the wire, plus staples and hammers. The three riders split up before they reached the boss of the HR. The two hands cutting left toward the bunkhouse, and Ty Schwinneger riding straight on to where his boss stood with his big head canted under his Stetson hat, squinting at his tough, bandy-legged foreman who, as he came closer, was obviously talking to himself. H.R. saw the lips moving, the anger in Schwinneger's posture. And as he so often did, he threw his ramrod off balance on meeting him. This time by smiling.

"Nice mornin'," HR said, his tone of voice fresh and easy. And he watched out of his one eye as Schwinneger dismounted, boiling.

"Nice for some maybe," Ty said. "You know the sign you put up on that cottonwood where the Stringers caught that rustler . . ."

"Gone? Is it?"

"Somebody wrote all over it."

"What did it say?"

The ramrod scowled even more now, for he'd been figuring on his boss sharing his anger. But HR didn't seem to care a damn one way or the other. He stood there whistling a ditty, very low, just between his teeth.

"The usual. Like the other times."

"We'll start the gather then. I got extra hands from the Stringers if we need them."

"Good enough. This waitin' around ain't what I like to do."

"You'll get your fill of the action right soon now," Rhodes said with a kind of grin.

"How soon d'you figure for the drive?"

"We'll begin pulling 'em in today. Right now. And I want the men to be armed. Everybody. Including Cookie."

"Cookie couldn't hit the side of a barn if he was holding it with one hand," the ramrod said.

"He ain't the only one," H.R. said, coming back fast. "But I want everyone packing hardware, and I want it to show."

He took out a cigar, but his foreman could see that there was no question of his being offered one. He didn't expect it. He wouldn't have liked it, for the matter of that, he told himself. One little touch of familiarity—like the other day—with his boss after all these years was good enough. No sense in overdoing such things. Ty Schwinneger felt better. He felt H.R. was more back to being his old self, which lately he hadn't been, and it hadn't been good. Now with the action, he could see it was like old times; more like when the range was freer, and there wasn't all the damn snivelling homesteaders and dirt farmers jamming up the country and messing with the range, the way they were doing more and more, each year more and more. And the old days were going. They were going fast. He sure didn't like that, and he knew H.R. for sure didn't either. Fact, there'd been a time when they'd used to talk about it, but then one day, it just stopped. Like there'd been nothing more to say. Ty didn't know which was worse, talking about it a lot, or never.

H.R.'s leg was good enough now so he could ride, and he'd had one of the men rope him out the new buckskin Stringer had sold him.

He mounted easily, his leg not hurting a bit, though he was stiff some. Buck tried to go into a crow hop or two, but H.R. kept his head up so he couldn't get it down low and buck.

There were six men with him now as they rode out. He told them to spread out and look everywhere, especially down in the breaks, and bunch whatever they found, loosely, on the back range.

"Then we'll have men checking the brands. I want each animal checked. And no mistakes. And Schwinneger—I want a true count."

Ty gave the orders to the men, the specifics, posted

outriders, and picked two of his older and more trust-
worthy hands to act as checkers. He didn't like working
with the Stringer men. First of all, you couldn't trust
them, and second, they didn't know cattle. But they
appeared to know guns, if not a helluva lot about
hosses. Still and all, they did what they were told.
And when he chewed one of them out for running his
horse downhill, the man took it. Old man Stringer had
instructed them well, it seemed. Well, good enough.
The damn crew weren't that much good at doing
anything else but follow what they were told.

By late afternoon they had the herd together. And
it seemed to Ty that even H.R. thought they'd done
a fair-to-good job. He'd had to straighten things out
a couple of times, but that wasn't too difficult. But
the more he worked with the Stringer men, the more
he was glad to have the HR men with him, men
who knew cows and horses, knew not to founder
their mounts, for crying out loud, or run the beef off
the cattle. And he gave himself credit, more than a
few times, for keeping his temper under control and
following H.R's orders real close.

"We'll be fixing to rest 'em this night," H.R. said
toward the end of the day. "And start moving 'em in
the early morn. First light'll do 'er, I reckon."

H.R. and his foreman stayed with the herd until it
was bedded down, the night guards posted, and the
outriders given their orders.

"I see you be takin' real care an' caution," Ty
observed as they had two steaming mugs of coffee
that Cookie brought into the main house just after
sunset.

"Man can't be too careful," H.R. replied. "With
the way things are." He took a good pull at his

coffee. "Can't be too careful," he repeated, his voice not quite in register, as though he was actually thinking of something else.

Ty Schwinneger waited.

Then: "How the Stringer men doing?"

"Good as you could expect it," Ty said.

"You get any trouble with a one of them, especially tomorrer, you cut the sonofabitch's balls off."

"I'd be happy to have a reason," the foreman said, his face and eyes grim.

H.R. nodded. "We're gonna get ourselves out of this hole we been in, my lad."

"With the bank."

"With the bank. With the goddam dirt farmers and homesteaders, with by God these damn fools who can't tell a cow from their own ass in broad daylight, but who're takin' over the country. Leastways they think they are . . . but they ain't, by God. They ain't gonna!"

He'd heard it all before. He'd said the very same. And Ty again asked the question. "Yeah, for sure. But how? How we gonna do that? Hell, we tried it with the hosses . . ."

"Keep your voice down, Goddammit!" And suddenly his boss had turned hard as a branding iron. "That was an idea somebody had. A notion. Steal hosses and change their markings and then accuse one of the nesters. Well, it ain't worked."

"I got a notion Stringer and his boys is still doing it," Ty muttered, not giving in to his boss's caution so easily. "Anyhow, there ain't no way a body could prove anything by now," he said, trying to get even with H.R's reprimand. "And besides, it didn't do that much good."

"It did enough good to get rid of more than a few of them nesters. Scared the shit out of 'em. Only thing is more come in. Goddamn them! Goddamn them to hell!" His face reddened, he fought with himself to keep his voice down. "Shit! Shit!" He spat furiously at a clump of sage. "Rustle us up some more arbuckle. Tomorrow, we'll settle the whole situation for good and all."

Except, he wasn't so sure about that. It had looked good, looked like things were working out, with Old man Stringer and his boys helping him—for the money of course; but mostly helping H.R. get rid of the sodbusters. But now that damn Soames had moved in. Him and the railroad and the land speculators, and what-the-hell-all. Soames. Sneaky like a goddam pack rat and twice as smart. The kind that played one side against the other. He, H.R., knew damn well that Soames had dealings with Stringer. And God knows who else.

Well, at any rate, he hadn't gotten euchred into anything bad. Though the sonofabitch had sure tried. Soames wanted the Bar Z what was more. Denzel's outfit. And God knows what all else! But for what? Not for running stock, not even for busting sod. But for selling land to the government, the foreigners, the new settlers, what the government called homesteaders. And likely to the railroad, that goddam thing that was spreading all through the country like a spider. Under the cover of bringing transportation and shipping possibilities to the cowmen and stockgrowers, they were in fact in the damn real estate business, running up the land values by creating county seats out of any old one-horse town, Things like that. Ruining the country. Bastards had no respect for who was

here first, and who built the land, civilized it, and
like . . .

Well, it had never been easy. And wasn't ever going
to be, by the looks of it. So a man just had to keep
going. A man—himself—who'd built something had
to keep going. The frontier for sure hadn't been won
by those assholes sitting at desks, lunching at the fancy
clubs in Denver and Cheyenne and all. Not a one of
them bastards had even heard a Injun war whoop scar-
ing the shit out of a man, by God. Not a one of 'em ever
faced cold steel or hot bullets. Or—shit—even fists.

He shook his head. He was feeling better by the
time Ty Schwinneger came back with two fresh mugs
of coffee. Ty—a good man. A top hand with the stock
and with the men too. A man he could count on.

And then again he found himself back into thoughts
of Emily, wishing she was here. Missing her. Thirty
years was a tight knot to cut through, by damn. And it
had been cut; there'd been nothing he could do about
it. Except wish it was different . . .

"That arbuckle sure talks back to a man, don't it,"
his foreman suddenly observed.

"Cookie's always sayin' a man needs a good stick
to start the day with," H.R. added.

"And come nighttime too," said Ty with a chuckle.

Ham Rhodes's mood lifted now. He was glad to
leave thoughts of Emily. Since her dying, he had
learned to handle it, but still it wasn't easy. The
worst was when he woke up at night and thought
of her. But this was rare. And right now he was able
to put her out of his mind. There was the herd to think
of, the outfit, and what the damn nesters and all were
doing to the country.

"You got anything on that Gunsmith feller?" he asked.

"What you mean?" Ty looked surprised at the question.

"I mean, have you heard anything on what he's up to. I know he ain't left the country. So something's got to be keeping him here."

"I know he's about," Ty said. "I know he checked for the Bar Z brand up around Buckskin Creek and down by the twin buttes, where we had most of the herd. Like he said he was going to do. You heard anything on what he might have found?"

H.R. shook his head. "Haven't. But I do expect to. He is not the kind of man to just pass over things. And he had to find something. That stupid sonofabitch Nevers who was using the running iron didn't know his ass from his whanger, dammit! But too late now for cryin'. I bin waitin' on Adams to show up. Besides, you know I tried to hire him onto the payroll to keep him quiet and also we could damn well use him."

"That is for sure," Ty Schwinneger said, nodding his head vigorously and blowing on his hot mug of coffee.

"I heard something about him maybe running for sheriff," H.R. said. "Sounds fishy to me."

"Sounds like somebody putting him up to it," Ty said.

H.R. nodded. "That's what I figured. Hell, Gilhooley's pretty well got that sewed up from what I hear."

They fell silent now, each with his own thoughts, while the sky darkened with the setting sun.

"I'd like to have another talk with that Adams," H.R. said finally. "Or . . ."

"Or what?" Schwinneger stared at him in the gray light. "What are you thinking?"

"I was thinking of maybe approaching Maggie Denzel. Hank and me had our troubles, but maybe she don't hold any grudge. Maybe it'd be helpful to them to have Adams working with us."

"Jesus!" His foreman was staring at him, with his mouth wide open. "You gone loco, have you? I thought we were going to run the herd right through the Bar Z."

"That's right," H.R. said. "That is what I had planned. But now suppose we *were* going to do that, but decided not to, on account of we want to help the small ranchers. Some of them leastways. Like the Bar Z. Then maybe we could get Adams to work with us."

"Work with us against the other small outfits? They'd never agree to that!"

"I know. I know." But Ham Rhodes was standing hard now, with his thumbs hooked into his belt, squinting at his foreman from under his wide brim. "I know it's late now, and we're all set with our first plan. But suppose we suddenly—suppose I suddenly rode over. Maybe even take you along with me, and said to them—Maggie and Johnnie and maybe that Gunsmith too that we wanted to join forces."

"Join forces for what?" Ty Schwinneger was almost dancing as he wobbled about scratching his head, his behind, sniffing, and spluttering at what he could only see as some crazy damn thing that had come over the boss. At the last minute! Crazy! The old geezer was losing his head!

But H.R. was looking at him cool as an evening wind. "You don't see it yet, do you, Ty."

And it was again being called "Ty," for about maybe
the second, third time since he'd known H.R. all this
while, that gave the tough little foreman pause. He
stood there in front of H.R. working his mouth as
though he had some tobacco or something stuck in
his teeth and couldn't get it loose.

"Don't you see it? That sonofabitch Soames. He's
been working things so that everybody around is
against everybody else. Not that it ain't easy as all
hell to be against Stringer. On account of I'd bet my
last dollar on him and his sons being right in with
Soames and his bunch. But see, Soames has gotten
everybody unsure so's he can just move in and take it
all while everybody's off balance and grabbin' leather.
Don't you see it now!"

He watched Ty Schwinneger's jaw drop.

"Holy shit!"

"That's right," H.R. said. "Holy shit. Like a kick in
the balls, my lad. And I'll bet there's more to it even.
I'll bet the sonofabitch is working on a lot more."

"Christ," the foreman said softly. "What are you
going to do then?"

"I dunno. But first I think we'll locate that Gunsmith
feller."

"But he didn't want anything to do with us."

"I know. That was then. This is now. And remember
we have got nothing to lose. We are in one helluva
tight fix. We knock off the Bar Z and move our herd
onto the top graze, then all we've actually done is
consolidate everything for Soames's bunch, who can
then move in with their gunmen, and bring the law
and peace, and set themselves in solid as Sunday
morning." He emptied his coffee mug and tossed it
to Schwinneger. "Tell the boys to hold the herd here.

I want to locate Adams and see what he has to say about this. It wouldn't surprise me if he didn't have it all figured out already, the smart sonofabitch."

In the early dawn, he lay quietly on his bedroll watching the silent light coming into the silent sky. The miracle was its simplicity, he realized suddenly. And he was at once filled with a sense of awe at the way nature was. How simple! How sure! And—yes—how responsible. And it offered no discussion, no argument. It was there. Simply there. No explanation was asked for and none was offered. Life, he realized, didn't have to have a reason.

And he was thinking how the Indian understood this. It was so simple. So clean. For everything that was needed—in the true sense of need—was right here all the time. Those so called savages understood this. And he realized that they lived what they understood. They killed game when it was necessary, and only then. And they made use of everything from innards to hide; even the claws were used. The entire buffalo was made good use of, either for food, clothing, shelter, or religious ornament. As it was in nature. How simple.

And there were times, such as now, when he felt this attitude very strong in him. Not that he wished to live like an Indian. After all, he was a white man, he was not red. He had not been raised in that way, that tradition. But he could learn from the Indian, as indeed he had over the years. But he was still of a different culture. He could honestly benefit from the advantages of each.

And right now, lying on his bedroll smelling his horse as he cropped the short buffalo grass he felt at peace, at ease and at one with the breathing of the sky, the land, and his whole body—his self.

He felt well rested and now allowed his thoughts to turn toward the Denzels and the trouble that was brewing on the range and in the town. It had frustrated him for this good while, he told himself, for while he could feel that there was trouble, he was in no way able to define it with any precision. It was too vague, too complicated, too—yes, devious.

But he had caught the smell of it, and the flavor. There was very definitely something wrong. And he knew it was something that Hank Denzel had stumbled on, and that it was, more than likely, why he had been killed.

But what exactly? Because he wouldn't sell his ranch? It was clear that pressure had been brought to bear on the various small stockmen. They'd been charged with rustling, horse stealing, switching brands. But it was also clear to Clint Adams that a whole lot of it had been planted by the big owners, men such as Ham Rhodes, claiming his stock had been rustled, re-branded, and that it was the small cattlemen doing it. By golly, it was the Johnson County War brewing all over again.

This time, though, the big stockgrowers had been more careful. They had again hired others to do their dirty work. Stringer, for sure, had taken that role. Stealing horses, changing markings with the paint brush while robbing and pillaging. Rebranding stolen cattle with the running iron. And the blame falling on the small outfits. On Hank Denzel.

But what was their purpose now? At the time of the Johnson County War the issue had been simple— graze. The small outfits were encroaching on the public range which the big stockmen considered theirs.

Now, there was a different reason for the struggle

against the small outfits. And what complicated it was
the fact that was at last obvious: there were different
motives. Some of the big ranchers still wanted to get
rid of the small cattlemen for the old reason—graze,
rangeland. But this time there was clearly some other
force at hand: some force that was not so concerned
with cattle and graze and open range, but rather with
the closing of the range into property, acreage that
could be sold and bought and resold. Acreage that
would be donated by the government in Washington
for the building of the railroad, the opening of the
frontier, and civilizing of the West.

And the reaping of profit. Great profit. Profit where
the life and death of towns and communities were
dependant on the plans and whims of men who had
come from somewhere else, men who didn't know the
land, had not worked it, lived on it, loved it. Men who
only saw the land as money. Men with connections in
the halls of politics in Washington, in San Francisco,
and in Chicago and Denver and New York and other
centers of finance. Thus, towns, communities were
born and died on the whims of finance and the drive
for power.

Yes, it was clear. A man such as Ham Rhodes
was fighting against the encroachments of the railroads, on the one hand, and on the other battling
the advances of the homesteaders and dirt farmers
and small stockgrowers. For the day of the free open
range, which they had benefited from, and fought and
died for; that day was gone.

Ham Rhodes knew this. He knew it all too well. But
a man on the order of Elijah Soames knew it better,
because such a man—and Soames was not singular:
there were others just like him—such a man was not

emotionally caught in the battle. His feeling was only for money and power. Whereas a Rhodes's feeling was for the land.

Clint fully realized however that a Rhodes did not share the feeling for land that the Indian held. His feeling for the land was the feeling of possessor; the Indian's feeling, Clint well knew, was as servant, caretaker, for the notion of owning nature was totally foreign to him.

He was rethinking all this again as he lay on his bedroll experiencing the movement of dawn and early morning. And at last he was able to see clearly how muddied the whole situation in and around Wingtree had become. In answering Hank Denzel's call, he had stepped right into a hornet's nest. He saw this clearly, and indeed, had suspected as much right from the beginning. Yet, he wouldn't have left where he happened to be right now for anything. Even though a white man, he shared something very basic with the Indian; he knew that the best place to be in one's life was right here, wherever he happened to be at a given moment. Right here and right now.

Thus, what had been right in front of him for some while, now became clear in the soft dawn of the day. And, as what he saw he had already known, but not quite acknowledged, became clear, he understood something he'd learned way back, something which at this particular moment invaded him with a suffusion of energy, clarity and the free sensation of total well-being. He understood that he was free to do what felt right in accordance with how he was now, in his feeling of a complete relationship with nature, the land around him, the sky, the air he was breathing. It was a sudden flash of a different kind of understanding, and it didn't remain in that very fine state. It left him. But there was a residue. A memory. And he knew it was there inside him, around him— somewhere. With it, he was experiencing the most extraordinary confidence. A confidence without a trace of arrogance or conceit, but with a certitude that what was going to happen would be correct. Not "right", not "wrong", in the ordinary sense of those words. But—once again—correct.

Now the sun was moving up above the horizon and the sky was all at once filled with gold. He looked over at Duke, who had suddenly raised his head from where he'd been cropping, and was now standing stock still, facing the rising sun.

Suddenly he remembered Hank's drawings-letter. Something had been pulling at him from those pictures, he realized now. He thought of the sketch of the hanged man, and how he'd come upon the man who had been lynched. And he realized suddenly that Hank had understood the situation that he, Clint Adams, had been unravelling in his thoughts and feelings. It fit perfectly. Hank's sketches had helped bring him toward his present understanding of the situation. Through the pictures, the feeling of something had come, and then bringing reason and common sense into it he had reached a new understanding, a completely fresh perspective.

Was this why Hank Denzel had been murdered? Hank must have somehow let it be known that he knew more, that he understood what—and maybe who?— was behind the trouble.

Reason enough to kill him. For Hank would have been quite open about his discoveries. He was that sort of man. Maybe he even confronted somebody, laid it on the line, and demanded to know what was going on.

Whatever he had done had earned him the abrupt ending of his life. And it had given the Gunsmith the message, and too, the means of finding out the truth. Maybe his friend Hank hadn't been killed so easily as his assassins had thought.

And yet—what? He knew there was something he wasn't seeing, but what? What had he missed? What was he not seeing?

He sat up on his bedroll now. And as he did so Duke, who had been standing stock still facing the rising sun, now dropped his head and returned to cropping the short buffalo grass.

Suddenly, without really giving it much thought, he reached into his possibles bag and pulled out Hank's letter and started to look again at his drawings. There was the Bar Z, there was the long, wide valley, and there was the hanging man. Nothing unusual, a horse thief caught and punished. And there was the cotton-wood tree from which he was hanged. And right at the roots, Hank's signature, and something that he took to be stones.

He had not really studied the picture before, being caught by the fact of the lynching of a horse thief. But now, he couldn't have said why, his attention was caught again by the half dozen or so, stones, or small rocks. They had little lines coming out from them, like the rays of a sun.

And suddenly, he realized what he was looking at. For he could have sworn that those rocks—or whatever they were—had not been there when he arrived on the scene.

TEN

Without a sound, without the slightest disturbance, morning stole into the little town. As it had ever since the first people had settled it. Suddenly a firecracker broke the cool silence. And when it was finished the quiet that returned seemed not the same. In that abrupt interference something had been lost.

A dog barked. Somewhere a window was thrown up. A door screeched open, and a man stood urinating behind his house. Cursing the last drop or two that got into his pants, he again opened the complaining door and entered his kitchen. He was greeted by the smell of strong, fresh boiled coffee.

Outside the No Return, a man lay on the boardwalk, half propped against the side of the building. He slept loudly within the ring of whiskey fumes surrounding him. The swinging doors suddenly pushed open and the swamper stepped out with his pail and mop, throwing the dirty water into the street.

"Go fuck yerself . . ." muttered the figure lying on the boardwalk.

"Still holdin' up the building, are you Bill," said the swamper, as he pushed back through the swinging batwings without a glance at the man who had told him to go fuck himself.

Down at the end of the street at the livery, a horse whickered as Old Link Arhammer walked through the line of stalls regarding his tenants, the half dozen horses who had spent the night. Off to his right a pack rat suddenly scampered to safety as the hostler's big feet and raspy breathing approached.

Standing in the wide doorway of his establishment, Link let his rheumy eyes wander up toward Main Street where he could see the steel-dust gelding hitched outside the Silver Dollar.

He glanced back behind him into the gloomy interior of the livery, and then looked back up Main Street. He was just in time to catch the man crossing from the Silver Dollar to the alley that ran alongside Jug's Eatery. Funny, how familiar he looked all of a sudden. For a minute he'd thought he was the one who'd ridden in on the steel-dust horse, but there was something different in his walk. Still, he'd come out of the Silver Dollar. Maybe the old eyes were getting older, he grumbled to himself and scratched along his forearm. When he turned back into the livery he knew he was no longer alone.

"Mornin', Mister Arhammer." The voice was soft, yet within that softness Link could hear, could feel the steel.

Link felt his throat tighten, but his voice was easy as he said, "What you want, Mister? You want a hoss?"

"I want you to just go about your business, and remember that I am right up here with this here, ready to cut you in two if you make any wrong move."

"Just tell me what to do, Mister. I ain't no hero. Just remember that."

There was something familiar in the voice, yet he couldn't place it. Not one of the Stringers, he was pretty sure of that. But he'd heard it somewhere. In the saloon, likely.

"Just go about your chores," the man in the loft said. "Don't do anything different. You got that."

"I do."

"Remember I be here."

"Make yerself to home, Mister. You want me to get you some coffee?"

There was just enough pause to tell the old hostler that he had scored.

"Just do your business. And cut the gabbing."

Link nodded and started down the aisle that ran the length of the livery between the two rows of stalls.

"Where you headin'?"

"Got to grain 'em," Link said. "Thought you told me to do my chores."

"Get to it then. Just don't do anything different is all."

"Then you best let me go for coffee up to Jug's. If I don't show up they'll figure somethin's the matter."

"You stay right here."

"What if somebody comes lookin'? I ain't trying to fool you, Mister, I do go up for coffee every morning. Every damn one."

"They come down lookin' for you, you'll handle it, remembering if you make a wrong move I'll blow your head off."

Old Link's Adam's apple pumped on that.

He got the can of oats and fed his charges. It didn't normally take very long, but he was spreading it out so that he'd have time to think. Evidently his visitor was waiting for somebody to brace or bushwhack. And the question was did he have others with him, either up in the loft or outside within firing range.

"How long has that big black gelding been here?" the voice asked.

"Come in last night. Like about sundown."

"Where's he stayin' at?"

"Who? The hoss? He is right here."

"You smart sonofabitch, I ast you a question. You got one second to answer it."

"I do believe he throwed his duffle at the Elk House."

Suddenly a shout and a firecracker came crackling in through the open doorway. A horse in the nearest stall jerked back in terror, nearly snapping its halter rope.

"What n' hell is that!" the voice in the hayloft demanded.

"Firecracker," Link explained. "The kids is up early. It's election this day."

"Shit! Scare the shit out of a stone statue that kind of shit!"

The old hostler said nothing to that, and the man above continued. "Who's getting elected, and for what?"

"Somebody to be sheriff," Link said.

"Shit! Thought we had a sheriff or marshal or whatever the hell he is. That Hooligan feller."

"Gilhooley," Link Arhammer said. "But he was temporary. Now they're gonna vote to make him permanent."

"Somebody goin' against him?"

"Dunno."

"Listen, Arhammer. You better shut up and do your work. Anybody comes in, you just act natural. You got that?"

"Yeah."

"Sure?"

"Who you looking for?"

"Never mind. You'll see."

"It ain't my business. Just thought I might help out if I knew who."

"Shut up now."

In the gloom of the stable Link Arhammer grinned. He recognized the voice now. It was the one named Simes, from the Stringer bunch, though he was also on loan out to Ham Rhodes's HR outfit. A small world, Link was thinking. But something in him was worried over the big black horse being there in the livery. Man such as Simes, well you wouldn't put it past him to do injury to a horse, especially a real good one like the black. And he wondered if the Gunsmith man was the one Simes was after. And whoever had sent him on the job? Who could that be? Old man Stringer? Or was it maybe Rhodes? He'd heard how the Stringer men now and again helped out when Rhodes was shorthanded.

And he was wondering too—why they would want to drygulch the Gunsmith fellow. What did they have against him. Only that he had a better horse than any one of them.

Well, he was known as the Gunsmith, and supposed to be lightning with that gun of his. But he felt sure he'd be along sooner or later, for he did keep a close check on the big black here at the livery when he was in town.

The old hostler stood in the doorway now facing the street and taking out a big chunk of chewing tobacco and his clasp knife, he cut off a generous piece and popped it into his mouth.

"You see anyone?" the voice called down.

Link took a step back into the entrance to the livery. "No."

"You're lying!"

"Then why'n hell you ask, fer Christ sake!" But he did get a turn wondering if he'd overstepped and was about to get air in his guts. He was trying desperately to think of something that would warn the Gunsmith, but also—and more important by far, was his getting out of what he'd stepped in. And right now.

He stood where he was, rooted into the ground, and yet strangely not overly worried. For he realized there was nothing he could do. Nothing anybody could have done. He knew if he called out to the man named Adams they'd both be shot dead by the man in the hayloft. So he did nothing. Maybe, just maybe he could . . .

As the man named Clint Adams, known as the Gunsmith, right now, walked into the Livery and Link Arhammer's mind went blank.

"The point to keep in mind, gentlemen, is that everything depends on getting rid of this man Adams." It was Elijah Soames delivering this important piece of information to the assembled council—Josiah Boles, Rock Hemming, and Tom Swindown—plus Acting Sheriff Random Gilhooley, who was on the very verge of being truly elected to the post of sheriff.

"Does everybody understand it?"

His hard eyes swept carefully over the assembled four, feeling for sincerity.

"Josiah?"

Josiah Boles cleared his throat. "Well, frankly, I'm not quite clear on just why Adams is so important— so vital if I understand you correctly—to our—uh— operation. All he appears to be is so called foreman to Denzel's outfit, which isn't of much account. I mean, apart from the fact that he also seems to be a disagreeable sonofabitch."

"The point is, he's dangerous," Soames said firmly. "It doesn't matter a damn how disagreeable he is, he is a menace. And he is also a man who can, could, and unless stopped, very likely, will cause big trouble."

"But how? I mean, unless he suddenly decides to run amok with his gun or something. I just don't see where he fits in?" Rick Hemming was staring in complete puzzlement at the man seated behind his desk in his office, which was still temporary, while the carpenters finished what would be his new, and grander place of business.

"Gentlemen. I must apologize." Soames held up the palm of his hand, to stay any apologies for even thinking of not understanding his plan. But he was enjoying himself vastly. He had them looped, by gosh, totally looped. Just the way he wanted them.

"You don't understand, gentlemen. Or rather—let me put it this way. I haven't made it clear." He leaned his elbows on the big table, pressed his palms together in front of his face, and said, "The difficulty with Adams, you see is simply that he is in the way. I believe he knows that. He is the foreman of the Bar Z. And the Bar Z is the lynch-pin to our enterprise." He lowered his arms onto the table, watching the surprise hit them.

"I know I haven't emphasized this."

The four faces were totally blank with surprise.

"You see, Adams is, was a friend of Henry Denzel, the—uh—departed owner of the Bar Z."

"And that means . . . ?" Josiah Boles cocked an eyebrow at the man on the other side of the big desk.

"That means he knows more about the, the—uh—situation than may be good for him."

"But how?" Hemming asked. "How could he? What could he know? Unless Denzel wrote him, or saw him. We're pretty sure he didn't see him, and we know Denzel didn't know how to write."

"And what would he tell him anyway?" Tom Swindown cut in. "That he had 250 instead of 275 head of cattle?"

"That I don't know," said Soames. "I have no idea what he could have told him, gentlemen. Except that the four of us here in this room know that the Bar Z is vital to the right-of-way of the railroad. They have signed a contract with me, and they will indeed run through Wingtree, thus putting Wingtree on the map. Very much! Why, I even see Wingtree as an excellent candidate for county seat." He paused. "But realize, whether or not you quite get the point—it is essential that this Gunsmith man be stopped. For consider—why does he have such a name? He is obviously a professional gunman. And Denzel hired him. Denzel was clearly planning to make trouble. And this man Adams is going to make trouble. Believe me!"

"He's been pretty quiet so far," Tom Swindown said. "Of course . . ."

"Of course he has been quiet," snapped Soames. "He's a gunman. A professional. He's biding his time and for all we know he may have us on his list. Remember Denzel hired him. And for what purpose? To kill. To kill who?" He stopped abruptly and looked at each one of them in turn.

"Who?" he repeated. "Which one of us will he target? Or will it be all four of you." His eyes fell on Random Gilhooley. "You are included, Sheriff."

His eyes played on them. He was holding their attention right in his hand, right on the tip of his tongue. Marvelous! He had them—and the town and outlying outfits right exactly and precisely—and without the slightest possibility of their escape, right where he wanted them! And all the aces were up his sleeve. All the aces including the one, the single big one!

Afterwards, when it was all over and done with, Link Arhammer said that it was too fast for one man to watch it. Never had he seen the like! Never! Two men to watch it, was what it would take. No question. At least two. One to see him reach, the other to see the loudmouth drop right out of that loft and land smack right at himself's feet!

Simes it was. Just like he'd reckoned. Dumb bastard was askin' for it. And not only fast! But accurate, by God. That Gunsmith; he had drilled that man right between the eyes! Nothing to it! Clean as a whistle, it was!

The Gunsmith had stood looking down at the man who had tried to out-gun him. He had already returned his six-gun to its holster.

"Well, it's started." Clint's words were quiet, barely audible to the hostler.

"Looks to me like you done finished it, mister."

"There is still the rest of it."

They had walked towards the tack room where the old hostler had coffee which he now offered his guest. "I keep some here 'case I don't get up to the cafe for my regular. Take sugar do you?"

Clint nodded, crossed the tack room to an upended crate and sat. "I believe he is one of Rhodes's men. Ran into him out at the HR."

"Was," said the hostler, correcting him wryly. "He belongs to the Lord or the Devil now—one."

Clint nodded, watching the old man boiling the coffee. "There're more where he came from."

"An' that's a gut," the old man said. He sniffed, took out the makings from his shirt pocket and built himself a smoke.

"You any notion why he was here?" Clint asked, accepting the mug the hostler handed him.

"Only that he or someone didn't take much to you, I'd say."

"I would never have figured that, Mister."

They both had a chuckle on that.

"He was also one of Stringer's men. Not family, but part of the gang." Link Arhammer had stuck his forefinger right into his mug of coffee to stir the sugar. Then licking his finger, he resumed his conversation. " 'Pears to me there'll be more after you. Would you say?"

"I would. They have got to the point where they figure I know something I shouldn't. 'Least that's how it is looking to me."

Link nodded. "Reckon."

"They think I know something, excepting I don't."

"Don't you even suspicion something."

Clint shook his head. "Nope. Yourself?"

"Only that I wouldn't try walking uptown right this day. I'd head for the horizon and right now, if I was you."

"Thanks for the advice." Clint stood up off the crate and put his mug on the shelf, from where the hostler had originally taken it.

"Like to offer you a hand, only I'm pretty stove up," the old man said.

" 'Preciate it."

Suddenly there was a silence between them. Clint was ready to leave, but he remained standing in front of the hostler. There was clearly more to be said.

It was Link Arhammer who spoke then. "You— you heading up the town then."

Clint nodded. "I ain't gonna find out which way the wind's blowin' settin' here picking my nose."

"You're a man who finds his share of trouble, it appears."

"I reckon I am." There was a quiet grin on the Gunsmith's face. He liked the old hostler. "I do appreciate your help, mister."

Link nodded.

Then—"Ever hear the name Anders?"

"I have."

"Then you heard what I said. Watch your back trail."

"Anything else?"

"Anders always packs extra help."

"I am not surprised. Lots of men carry extra—just in case."

The old hostler cut his eye to the door, then looked back at Clint who was standing. "You know them Stringer twins, Matt and Harvey?"

"I've run into them."

"Can you tell 'em apart?"

"I can, though I don't know their names. I studied them, the way they moved."

"People can't tell one from th'other."

"I can," Clint said.

"Good enough then. I wanted to be certain."

And he nodded as Clint waited to see if there was more, but there wasn't. Their conversation was ended on that strange note.

The sun was high now. And hot. But for an election time, Clint noted the Main Street seemed pretty empty. He wondered if people were actually voting, the result apparently being such a foregone conclusion. The excitement for the election had been small to begin with, and even though certain elements had tried to whip something up, like the news that Mister Elijah Soames was not voting for Gilhooley— to everyone's astonishment—things had really tapered off. A foregone conclusion had been accepted. Manipulation, the Gunsmith noted to himself, had again played its hand. And he knew that all the game-playing about who was going to be sheriff, and when and where, and even if the railroad was coming to Wingtree, was all handling, manipulating; the real story was well hidden but was being played out nonetheless.

Right now the street was nearly empty, though he knew that the townspeople weren't still asleep in bed. On the contrary, the very atmosphere seemed to vibrate with an anticipation. And as he walked down the boardwalk toward the No Return Clint Adams began to feel it more.

At the same time he could see the action in various alleys, and along the roof lines of some of the buildings. And he wondered where the play would be made—indoors or out in the street. And now his thoughts centered on Anders. All he knew of the man was that he was a hired killer, working mostly for the stockgrowers. Thus, he could be here on behalf of Ham Rhodes, or it could be somebody else. He wondered just what role Elijah Soames was playing. It seemed evident that he was connected with the railroad in some way, but mostly with the buying and selling of lots, where the big profit lay.

For a while he had wondered whether Soames would approach him again with some deal or other, and when he didn't he realized that he was now the target. Soames was the type who said if you can't work with them then get rid of them.

The question now was how. Clint realized that Link Arhammer had been trying to give him a warning. He'd mentioned the Stringer twins. Did that mean they were gunning for him? And why had he asked him if he could could tell them apart?

Now he was just outside the No Return. Surely they wouldn't make a play in the saloon. But they would be clever, he knew. And by now they would know about Simes and they'd be doubly cautious, but also very likely, more bold at the same time. Because this would be the big play that would decide everything. The way, of course, would be the way of distraction. They would attempt to pull his attention away from the serious action. That, after all, was the basic method in this kind of fight. Outrageous surprise . . .

The No Return was almost deserted. The batwing doors made a strange, echo-like sound as he pushed them open and they flew back after he'd passed through.

The light was dim after the bright street, but his eyes quickly adjusted. There were men at the bar, but they weren't really drinking. They were, he immediately saw, all cut from the same mold. But he was counting on the fact that Elijah Soames was a theatrical person. He liked style. He was not a man to do things in a small way. And what's more, he was a gambler. It was not his style to have a half dozen men gun someone down. Especially someone with a reputation, a man like himself. No. He would favor a contest, a drama. Thus—Anders. But of course . . .

But where was Anders? He was halfway into the quiet room when a voice spoke from the bar.

"Well, if it ain't the Gunsmith. Fellers, this here is the one who thinks he's the fastest gun alive. Take a good look."

"You want something from me, mister?" The Gunsmith had stopped and spoke quietly into the now very still, almost silent room.

"Just saying hello, Gunsmith. See, I ain't armed."

He had already noted that nobody was packing hardware. Yet, the atmosphere seemed more threatening than if they'd all been armed.

But where was Anders?

He heard the door of the back room open, heard the steps walking slowly toward the big open area in front of the long bar.

Clint's searching glance had been taking in the balcony that ran along two sides of the room, and which housed the cribs where the girls did their business. There was no action there. But where was Anders?

And then he heard the steps stop, but the sound came from the far end of the bar, where a small bunch of men stood. He saw no one extra there who might have just joined the group. Then he heard more steps, and this time he saw the big man detach himself from another group of men to his right at the other end of the long bar.

"Gunsmith."

The voice was hard, guttural. And he knew it was Anders. He could see something of a movement in the small group off to his left. And then, looking in the big mirror behind the bar he detected movement at the opposite end.

"You looking for somebody, Gunsmith?"

"Reckon I'm looking for you, mister."

"Name's Anders, Gunsmith. And I'm right here."

In the mirror he saw the man leave the group at his left. And in that moment he remembered Link Arhammer's remark about the Stringer twins, and could he tell them apart.

In the next second he had stepped instantly out of the line of fire, where he was zeroed between two opposite ends of the long bar. He was looking right at Anders now, and at the same time, seeing in the mirror another Anders—a double, an identical Anders at the far end of the bar. Both wearing handguns.

In that shaved second the Gunsmith's hand swept his Colt from its holster and drilled the man named Anders, standing to his left, right through the heart. At the same time—even swifter, almost seeming as though the second bullet had overtaken and passed the first—he fired again, this time catching the other Anders in the throat.

"God almighty," somebody murmured, as Clint removed his Stetson hat and readjusted it on his head.

The two bodies lying on the floor each had a single bullet hole—one in the heart, the other in the throat.

He stood in the center of the barroom now, having holstered his six-gun.

"Anybody else have something to say?"

Not a sound could be heard. The room was barely breathing.

"That's enough now. The Anders boys have pulled that stunt of theirs before. I almost forgot for a minute that Anders was two. But somebody reminded me."

He was looking at Heavy Harry the bartender as he spoke.

Harry nodded. "The drink is on the house, Mister. All you want. With my personal thanks, lemme add!"

Someone unknown said a weak "Hear-hear!" And the room resumed its life, though now, it seemed, at a slower, refreshed pace.

When Clint Adams got back down to the livery, he found his saddle gear all laid out and ready for him. And so was Duke.

"Be riding on, will you?" the hostler asked.

"After a spell maybe."

The old man hid his grin. "Good to have you about, sir. I wouldn't bet on it, on account of I ain't a bettin' man, but I'd sure pree-dict it, that the boys'll simmer down now."

"Reckon," Clint said. When he'd mounted Duke he touched the brim of his hat to the old hostler.

"Mister Gunsmith, I mean Mister Adams, sir. You look to me like the cat what swallered the canary."

"Just remembered that a canary's color is gold." And he walked Duke out of the big barn and into the clear daylight.

"Holy shit! You mean to tell me that there's . . . !"

"Maybe."

"Is that what Soames was after?"

"It was."

"You're saying he don't know where it's actually at, but you do."

"You said it."

"And you ain't telling."

"You said it again."

"I take it you ain't interested in gold yerself."

Clint grinned at the old man. "Go to the top of the class," he said. And he nodded and kicked Duke into a fast walk and then into a canter.

Not very long after he was looking into the eyes of Hank Denzel's deliciously endowed daughter. Johnnie Denzel, as their great good fortune had it, was out with the stock. And his sister and the Bar Z ranch foreman had lost no time in getting together.

At one resting point during their delightful encounter, Miss Denzel asked the Gunsmith what had happened, and he told her.

"But how did you know that it was about gold, and not the railroad or something else like cattle or land?"

"Oh, it's about cattle too and very much about land," Clint said. "But the gold is there too, as a bonus; I should say, 'here,' since it's on your land. The Bar Z. Except only Soames knows it."

She looked surprised. "But how come nobody else knows it?"

"Because I won't tell them," he said. "And Soames—well, it won't do him any good to know about it now, simply because we also know."

"But how did you ever find out that there was gold?"

He grinned at her, as he stroked his finger very lightly in her belly button. "By studying your dad's pictures, his drawings. You know the old saying about a picture being worth a thousand words, or something or other."

"How about a thousand kisses, sir?"

"On one condition," the Gunsmith said.

"What's that?"

He leaned down and whispered into her ear.

"Mister Adams! Do you really think we could do it that many times!"

"I know a good way to find out," the Gunsmith told her.

Watch for

THE VENGEANCE TRAIL

120th in the exciting
GUNSMITH series
from Jove

Coming in December!

If you enjoyed this book, subscribe now and get...

TWO FREE

A $7.00 VALUE–

If you would like to read more of the very best, most exciting, adventurous, action-packed Westerns being published today, you'll want to subscribe to True Value's Western Home Subscription Service.

Each month the editors of True Value will select the 6 very best Westerns from America's leading publishers for special readers like you. You'll be able to preview these new titles as soon as they are published, *FREE* for ten days with no obligation!

TWO FREE BOOKS

When you subscribe, we'll send you your first month's shipment of the newest and best 6 Westerns for you to preview. With your first shipment, two of these books will be yours as our introductory gift to you absolutely *FREE* (a $7.00 value), regardless of what you decide to do. If

you like them, as much as we think you will, keep all six books but pay for just 4 at the low subscriber rate of just $2.75 each. If you decide to return them, keep 2 of the titles as our gift. No obligation.

Special Subscriber Savings

When you become a True Value subscriber you'll save money several ways. First, all regular monthly selections will be billed at the low subscriber price of just $2.75 each. That's at least a savings of $4.50 each month below the publishers price. Second, there is never any shipping, handling or other hidden charges—*Free home delivery*. What's more there is no minimum number of books you must buy, you may return any selection for full credit and you can cancel your subscription at any time. A TRUE VALUE!

J.R. ROBERTS
THE
GUNSMITH